SUNNY MATES AND MURDERS

A RAINA SUN MYSTERY

ANNE R. TAN

To my dad,
for always making me feel like
I'm your favorite child.

1

ANOTHER PROPOSAL

Raina wrinkled her nose at the rotten vegetable and slight sewer odor and pushed open the glass door into the chop suey shop in the seedier part of the Chinatown in Toronto, looking for a man with a silvery scar on the side of his face. The Chinese triad boss had suggested this mid-morning rendezvous, which meant he had been keeping tabs on her since their unfortunate meeting earlier in the year. If he hadn't stolen her deceased grandfather's journal, she would have stayed on the opposite side of the continent. People who got involved with organized crime didn't enjoy healthy lives.

"You see him?" Po Po asked in a stage whisper.

Raina sighed, regretting the decision to bring her grandma along. "I would be blind to miss him," she replied not even bothering to lower her voice. By him, she meant Sonny Kwan, the Dai Lo of the Nine Dragons triad. The literal translation for Dai Lo was Big Brother, the formal title for the leader of a Chinese criminal organization.

The restaurant was long and rectangular and about the size of a cargo container. Along one wall was a stainless steel counter with strips of barbecue pork, steamed chicken, and roast pig hanging from the rail above it. The cook with a clean apron picked his nose while watching his two customers. A Hispanic woman at a nearby table fiddled on a cell phone. Her focus on the small screen in front of her meant she was hyper-aware of their arrival. She had to be his henchwoman. After all, what self-respecting criminal boss would leave home without one?

Raina's pulse jumped at the sight of Sonny slurping a steaming bowl of wonton noodle soup at the rear of the restaurant. The last and only time she'd seen him, Sonny wore an ill-fitted outfit he had stolen from a laundromat because he got blood—not his—all over his clothes.

Today, he was in a silk short-sleeve shirt and designer ripped jeans. His black hair was longer and tied at the nape of his neck into a short ponytail. She could imagine him tossing his hair back like a Chinese version of Fabio in the bedroom. The silvery scar on the side of his face added to his roguish pirate vibe some women might find titillating.

Raina took a deep breath, hoping to calm herself. The henchwoman posed a dilemma she hadn't thought of when she agreed to this tête-à-tête. A man like Sonny might allow certain liberties in private—especially with a family debt between them—but he would shoot her first before losing face in front of his associates.

She poked her grandma in the ribs and tipped her chin at Sonny. "It's show time."

Po Po glanced at the flower broach on Raina's blouse. It hid a microphone. "You got the earpiece on?"

Raina smoothed her curly black hair against her ear to cover the clear plastic earpiece that would allow her grandma to listen in on her conversation with Sonny.

"Are you sure you want to do this?" Po Po asked. Her voice held a tinge of anxiety.

Raina glanced at her beloved grandma. Since Po Po had found out her deceased husband had a secret family with another woman, she hadn't had a good night's sleep, often roaming her condo complex in the dead of the night. Her face, once a rural roadmap, became transit lines in a crowded city. What woman could rest easy when fifty years of marriage turned into one fat lie?

"We need the journal." Raina answered. *And you need to know why your husband married another woman in China.*

Po Po's smile wavered, and she patted Raina's cheek. "You are a good girl, Rainy. I'm so lucky you still want to spend time with your granny."

Raina swallowed the lump in her throat and glanced around. Everyone in the restaurant watched them. She had a feeling they all knew what was going on, but played along anyway like she did for her grandma's sake.

Po Po planted herself next to the henchwoman and pulled out her cell phone. "You play Pokémon Go?" she asked the Hispanic woman.

The henchwoman scowled and shifted her body to put more space between the two of them. Her grandma scooted closer, holding out the display of her cell phone.

Raina meandered around the small tables and made her way towards Sonny. She pulled out a chair and sat across from him.

"Want anything to eat?" Sonny asked, pointing a finger at the cook. "It's on the house."

Raina shook her head. Did the Nine Dragons use the restaurant as a front for their criminal activities? It didn't matter. She wasn't here to figure out how his organization worked. "Thanks for taking the time to meet with me." Her voice stumbled over the stiff words.

For all she knew, Sonny could shuttle her into a human trafficking ring with no one blinking an eye. Her bird-like grandmother couldn't even deter a hungry cat, so there would be no help from that direction. Not that Raina would want to put Po Po in danger. It would take more than charm to get her grandfather's journal back, and Raina had little in the way of collateral.

Sonny raised an eyebrow, and his lips curled in one corner. "Are you always this formal when you let one of your boyfriends spank you?"

Raina held up both palms. "Whoa! There will be no spanking here unless you want to bend over my knees."

"Okay. We could have pillow talk afterwards."

Raina didn't want to be in a closed room with a known triad boss. What if he handed her a ping-pong paddle? "You're spoiling the bad boy image in my mind."

"Would you rather I threaten to drag you into a prostitution ring instead?"

Her eyes widened at hearing him echo her earlier thoughts. Trusting a fifty-year-old family debt to keep him aboveboard was like trusting a toddler to choose carrots instead of cake.

"I don't bite pretty women"—he paused, smirking—"unless they ask me too."

Raina pointed at herself. "Not asking here."

"My make-up kisses are worth it though." He chuckled at his one-sided joke. "You have my word—I won't let anything happen to you as long as you're with me."

She studied the amusement in his dark brown eyes. The scar on the side of his face didn't mar his attractiveness. At another place and time, they might be friends.

"Sorry to disappoint you, but it won't happen. Do you want your associates to listen in on our conversation?"

Sonny gestured at his cronies. "Cat, you can keep an eye on things outside. Hey, Cook, time for a break."

With a scrape of the chair on the cracked tile floor, the henchwoman got up. She flicked her eyes between Sonny and Raina and strolled outside with a scowl. The cook popped a cigarette into his mouth, nodded at Raina, and then strolled past them and banged open the back door.

Sonny glanced back at Raina. "What about your grandmother?"

"Who?" Raina focused on the spot between his eyes.

"The old lady who's trying to take photos of us with her cell phone. Does she like to watch spy movies?"

"Cop shows," Raina mumbled.

"Why am I not surprised? Now what can I do for you, Rainy?"

"Raina. We're not close enough for you to call me that."

Sonny scooted his chair closer until his knees touched hers underneath the table. "I can get even closer if you let me."

Raina ignored his comment. Men like Sonny put on this flirting act only to make women squirm. He didn't need to know she was anything but perfectly at ease. She shifted her legs, kicking him in the shin. "Sorry. You know how clumsy I am."

He shifted his legs so they were no longer touching. "Your hair is longer. I like the new look."

"Where's my grandfather's journal?" Raina asked, tired of their stupid game. "Just give it back and we're squared. I'll never mention the debt your family owes mine again."

"We're already squared. Did you think your grandfather built his international shipping business on his own? In the sixties when racism was the norm? Without the drug money and muscles from the Nine Dragons I doubt your family would have enjoyed these decades of prosperity."

Her family never spoke of the earlier days when they were new immigrants. She had assumed the seed money from her Po Po's inheritance had multiplied with hard work.

"I could threaten to reveal how my grandfather saved yours to your men"—he stiffened at her words—"but I'm not looking for a swim at the bottom of a lake. Without the information in the journal, my grandma would spend her remaining years dragging a broken heart around. This might shorten her life." Her voice choked up, and her gaze drifted to her grandma who was busy snapping photos of the restaurant like she wanted to document her last moment.

"I didn't say I wouldn't give the journal back. I need you to help me out first," Sonny said.

She narrowed her eyes at him. "I'm not making

another bargain with you. The last time you didn't keep your end of the deal."

"If I'd stayed—" Sonny made a slicing motion underneath his chin. "You can't blame a guy for skipping town."

It was hard to reconcile the suave educated man with the hardened criminal underneath. When he wanted to charm, it was easy to ignore the scar on the side of his face and the weapons he undoubtedly hid on his person. "Where did you go to college?"

"What makes you think I'm not your average thug?"

"If you want to play stupid, that's fine with me."

One corner of his lips curled in amusement. "Stanford."

"You didn't stay local? University of Toronto is a good school."

He shook his head. "Too close to home. I wanted to get away from the Nine Dragons."

She raised an eyebrow. "You did a fine job. Seeing as how you're the boss and all now."

He chuckled. "Yeah, I did. Look, you want your grandfather's journal, and I need a fiancée for this weekend. Come to my house party as my fiancée, and I'll give you the journal when you leave."

Raina studied the brown eyes. He appeared relaxed and sincere. "What's the catch? Are you going to shuttle me into a human trafficking ring? Or is this a Playboy party where I'm expected to give out favors?"

Sonny held her gaze. "I do a lot of things, but forcing women into prostitution is not one of them. You are safe with me. Are we clear on this?"

She nodded.

He flicked a glance at her chest. "And your girls are not big enough to tempt me."

"At least they're natural," Po Po whispered in Raina's ear.

Raina jumped, her leg kicking Sonny again.

He scooted his chair back. "Will you watch it?"

"Sorry." Raina had forgotten her grandma was listening to their conversation. She ignored both comments about her bra size. "Why do you need a fiancée? Are you trying to make someone jealous? Even when I clean myself up, I'm not much of a looker."

"Yes, you are," Po Po whispered into her ear.

"I didn't bring any fancy clothes," Raina said, ignoring her grandma again.

"We can go shopping later," Po Po whispered. "Say yes."

Raina bit her lip to stop from snapping at her grandma. Holding two conversations at the same time was distracting.

"Don't worry about it. Cat can pick up a few dresses for you," Sonny said.

"I don't want to look like a slut," Raina said.

"If I wanted a slut, I could bring one of the girls I party with. I need someone with a little more class."

Raina snorted. Class? Her? "Do I get my own room?"

"No."

"Do I get my own bed?"

"I'd share a bed with him," Po Po said.

Raina's cheeks burned. She should have left her grandma at home.

Sonny didn't seem to notice her divided attention. "You can show up with a chastity belt for all I care."

"Why me?" Raina asked.

He tugged at a dangling curl on the side of her face. "I want to get to know you better."

Raina batted at his hand. "Stop pretending to flirt with me."

Footsteps pounded at the entryway. Raina whirled around, her heart leaping to her throat. Cat rushed into the restaurant, her gun drawn.

Raina held both hands in the air. "Whoa!"

Po Po screamed, dropping her phone.

"Ouch!" Raina's hand flew to her ear. She grabbed the earpiece and shoved it into her pocket.

"What do you think you're doing?" Sonny snapped at the henchwoman.

Cat lowered the gun, her eyes flicking from her boss to Raina. "I thought I saw a rat." She tucked the gun back into the shoulder holster underneath the shrug she wore over her tight tank top.

Sonny tipped his chin toward the door. "Get out of here." After Cat left, he asked Raina, "Are you okay?"

Raina nodded even though her heart hammered in her chest, but she kept her face expressionless.

"You don't look fine," Sonny said. A thug waving a gun must be an everyday occurrence in his life.

"I almost wet my shorts," Raina said, her voice a decibel higher than normal. "Is this what you want to hear?"

"A gun is nothing compared to the dead bodies you seem to attract."

"A dead body is no threat to my safety," Raina said, her heartbeat slowing down from its earlier spike. "I'm not sure spending a weekend with your family and associates will be good for my heart."

"I promise there will be no hanky-panky this weekend," Sonny said. "My ex will be at my grandfather's birthday party. She left me at the altar, but I'm over it. I want my family to know I have moved on."

Raina suppressed a smirk. *Oh, he was so not over this ex.* "Just don't get me an orange-colored dress, and you got yourself a deal." She held out a hand.

Sonny shook it and smiled. "Now I have something to look forward to."

Po Po did a fist pump.

Sonny's gaze flicked to her grandma. "Just don't bring her."

Raina ignored the tingle of anticipation settling into her stomach. "I don't plan to."

She didn't want to worry about her grandma if Sonny turned out to be a liar. Neither did she want to risk her grandma wrecking the tenuous bargain between her and Sonny. She was getting her grandfather's journal back, and this time, nothing would stand in her way.

2

MY KINGDOM FOR A CLOCK

The next morning Raina and her grandma were having breakfast at their furnished two-bedroom vacation rental within walking distance to the Chinese Cultural Centre and the office for the Chinese Opera Company.

"For the last time, you're not coming with me," Raina said. Why did she mention her summer plans to her grandma? She could have flown to Toronto on her own to deal with Sonny.

"Are you sure I can't come with you? I could play the role of the grand dame. I won't embarrass you in front of your fiancé's family," Po Po said.

"First, Sonny is not my fiancé. Second, you're my lifeline in case I need someone to bust me out." Raina doubted her grandma could help if she were shuttled into an underground lair, but it made Po Po feel useful, and most important of all, kept her out of harm's way.

"What if this was just a ruse to get you alone?"

"If it is, you can come rescue me with guns blazing."

Po Po narrowed her eyes and stalked into her bedroom. She didn't quite slam the door, but it was enough for Raina to know she was in the doghouse.

Raina sighed, trying to let the tension out. She didn't expect it would be easy to get her grandfather's journal back, but neither did she expect it to take much effort. She had hoped for a short two-week stay in Toronto and then she could go back to her life in Gold Springs, California. Instead, it took almost three weeks for Sonny to even answer her messages. This fake fiancée gig might be her only chance, and she didn't want to blow it.

Po Po returned to the kitchen table with a pair of hair sticks and a silver ID bracelet with a stamped orchid pattern on the flat plate where a name would typically be engraved. "There's a GPS tracker on the bracelet. It'll go well with your outfits."

Her grandma often pretended to be Q, supplying Raina with weapons of mass destruction. Sometimes her toys were wacky, but a few had saved Raina's life on more than one occasion.

Raina slipped the bracelet onto her wrist. "It's pretty. Thanks."

Po Po whirled her silver braid into a knot on the back of her head, using the hair sticks to hold it in place. The charms from the end of the hair sticks jingled when her grandma shifted her head. "Pretty, but deadly." She pulled a stick out of her hair and jabbed the pointed end at Raina's face.

Raina scooted back and almost fell off the chair. "You could have poked my eyes out."

Po Po beamed. "Exactly! Or you can ram this in his throat or crotch." She tapped on the hair stick. "Titanium. I had it specially made for us." She pointed at the butterfly's antennae on one of the charms. "You can pick a lock with this."

"What about the other charm? What does it do?" Raina asked, leaning in closer to have a look at the orchid flower.

"If you press the leaf here, it becomes a flashlight. The semi-precious stones camouflage the LED bulb."

Raina hugged her grandma. "Don't worry, I can take care of myself."

The rest of the day was spent getting ready for the upcoming weekend. They stopped by the Chinese herbal shop to get a variety of expensive teas for a birthday present. If she showed up empty handed to the party, it wouldn't take a genius to guess something was off in the engagement.

By the time Raina crawled into bed, she was beat, but she still ended up tossing and turning most of the night. She woke up with the sun and went for a morning run. The next two days would be spent feasting and lounging around like a pampered lapdog.

She returned to the rental, showered, and typed an email to Matthew Louie—whose proposal she'd turned down a few weeks ago. If she "disappeared," this ex-Marine could find her. She scheduled the email for Monday, giving herself plenty of time to delete it if all went as planned.

A limo arrived after breakfast. The driver loaded Raina's overnight bag into the vehicle and she was off, heading to the small town of Aurora. The drive was uneventful, and she drifted off until the car stopped in front of wrought iron gates. When the driver clicked a button on the roof of the vehicle, the gates opened.

Raina's breath caught in her throat. Rolling green lawns, a sparkling lake, and an old mansion. She didn't know the architectural style for the mansion, but it could have been a set for *Pride and Prejudice*. Normal people didn't live in homes like this. A thrill of excitement ran through her. She could imagine dancing on the terrace under the moonlight with a Mr. Darcy during the birthday party.

As the limo rounded a bend, a guard shack came into view. Raina couldn't see through the tinted windows. A mounted security camera underneath the eaves pointed at the gate. As they cruised up the winding drive-way, she saw more security cameras mounted on the trees. A man walking several Dobermans stopped to let them pass. Guard dogs.

Raina shivered and turned away from the window. By the time the driver pulled up to the house, several people waited for them next to the double front doors. A footman opened the car door and closed it after Raina got out. He grabbed her bag from the trunk and headed toward the house.

Sonny came down the steps to greet her. "Thanks for showing up," he whispered into her ear. "Come meet my older brother and his wife. You'll meet everyone else at dinner."

He led her up the steps toward the Chinese couple in their late-thirties. The brother had the placid face of someone used to hard living or endless partying. The woman had the dejected expression of a long-suffering wife. If an unhappy marriage had a look, this was it.

A flutter of butterflies settled in Raina's stomach. Why did the leadership go to Sonny? The Nine Dragons must have a strict power structure where the leadership went from father to the eldest son like most Chinese families. Did she have to worry about Jerry and his supporters this weekend, too?

"Raina, this is my brother, Jerry, and his wife, Lily," Sonny said, placing a hand on the small of her back and propelling her forward.

Jerry flicked a glance at Raina, sweeping from head to toe, and raised an eyebrow. "How much is he paying you this weekend? I'll triple it so I don't have to watch the charade."

Lily gasped. "Jerry!"

"We both know she's a high-class hooker here to make Myling jealous," Jerry said.

Sonny's face flushed, turning into a shade of eggplant. The silver scar on the side of his face stood out. "How dare—"

Raina burst out laughing, throwing her head back. Her a high-class hooker? Yeah, if a man wanted a scrawny Chinese girl with hair like a bird's nest.

All three of the Kwans gaped at her.

"Sorry, I'm just not used to the compliment," Raina said. "Usually I'm the one who would have to fork over the big bucks for Mr. Hotshot." She slapped Sonny in the butt. "Why don't you show me the bedroom so you can ravish me as promised before dinner?"

Lily jumped at the sound. "Um, yes... It's a good idea to settle in first. We'll have plenty of time to get to know each other."

"Where is the ring?" Jerry asked, his voice heavy with doubt.

"I'm just too picky. We've visited several jewelry stores, but I can't seem to find anything that's my style," Raina said. She shrugged one shoulder. "It has to be the right one."

Sonny took a deep breath. As the flush left his face, his eyes twinkled with amusement.

Jerry glowered at them. "Whatever. Myling will eat you for breakfast, girl."

Raina beamed at Sonny, ignoring Jerry's comment. "I need to thank her. If Sonny didn't come out to San Francisco after she left, I would never have met him."

Score one for Sonny, Raina thought. Would she be subject to verbal combats between the brothers all weekend?

Sonny nodded at his brother, grabbed Raina's hand, and led them upstairs. At the landing area, he whirled around and thoroughly kissed Raina. He broke off the kiss as suddenly as he started it.

"You were fantastic. I knew you were the right girl for this," he said.

Raina wiped her mouth with the back of her hand. "Keep your hands and your mouth to yourself when we are not performing. I should get hazard pay for this."

"What happened to friends with benefits?"

"We're not friends."

He pressed his hands to his heart like she had wounded him. "Ah! You hurt me."

Raina took a step toward him. "I can make it worse. Now where's my grandfather's journal?"

He waved a finger. "Not until tomorrow morning."

"Why is your ex coming to this party?"

The amusement left his face. "She's now married to Freddie Low, the Dai Lo for the Black Tiger triad in New York City. They are coming to pay their respects to my grandfather and to cash in a favor. They are having problems with the Italian mob, and they want our help."

Raina shivered and turned to look outside the window at the rolling green lawns. A whole weekend surrounded by criminals that would give Matthew a heart attack? And a power struggle between Sonny and his brother Jerry? This was a much deeper game than she'd expected.

RAINA FROWNED at the image in the full-length mirror in the bedroom suite. The magenta silk dress looked fabulous, except when she looked down at her chest. The cups built into the bust area were too big for her petite frame. Every time she shifted, the material bunched into unattractive indentations. She didn't know whether she should be flattered or offended that Sonny thought she could fill out the dress.

As she marched to the bathroom, the charms on the hair sticks in her chignon jingled merrily. She grabbed the roll of toilet paper and marched back to the mirror. It had been years since she felt the need for padding, but what was a girl to do in this situation? She stuffed the toilet paper in her chest, shifted the wads until they looked natural, and hoped they didn't drop out when she leaned in to sip her soup. This would make a wonderful impression on Sonny's ex.

Raina grabbed her evening bag and stepped into the hall. Showtime. The hubbub of conversation drifted toward her the closer she got to the stairs. Yikes! She was supposed to be in line with the rest of the Kwan family to greet the arriving guests. She trotted as quickly as the three-inch heels allowed, swaying like an elephant on stilts. Down the hall, down the stairs, and across the foyer.

Jerry, Lily, and Sonny stood by the front door—smiling, nodding, and shaking hands with people. The brothers ignored each other, and the grandfather was MIA. Raina would probably meet the patriarch of the family during dinner. Lily's smile was brittle, and she played with the beads on her gold dress whenever she didn't have to speak to anyone. Playing referee between the two brothers must be exhausting.

For the next forty minutes, Raina smiled and nodded like Miss Universe on steroids. While there was no open hostility from the guests, she could sense an underlying tension among Nine Dragons senior members. The handful of family ignored the men from the triad and banded together like sheep surrounded by a wolf pack.

Sonny stiffened, and Raina followed his gaze to the couple coming in through the front door. Must be the ex and her new husband, Myling and Freddie Low. Jerry and Lily stepped up to greet the couple, and an aunt came over to pinch Sonny's cheek. He pointedly ignored the Lows. Disaster averted.

Raina shifted so she could see the ex.

Freddie Low said something and wrapped a protective hand on his wife's back. Jerry reacted as if Freddie threw a glass of water on his face. His head jerked back, and he turned ashen.

Lily glanced at Sonny, but caught Raina's eyes, and averted her gaze. She pasted a stoic smile on her face, but the lights weren't on inside the house.

Myling blushed and placed a hand on her flat stomach. The corners of her lips curled into a satisfied smile like a cat who lapped up all the cream.

Raina's eyes widened. *Is Myling pregnant?*

The aunt moved on, and another couple came to shake Sonny's hand. By the time Raina glanced over at Jerry and Lily again, the Lows had disappeared into the ballroom. Sonny appeared relaxed, but Raina was afraid of his reaction when he heard of Myling's pregnancy.

Eventually, everyone went in the ballroom for drinks and appetizers.

Raina wiggled her toes. "I hope you appreciate my sacrifice for being your eye candy. My back is killing me in these shoes."

Sonny glanced down at her feet. "Why don't you change into something more comfortable?"

"Are you sure?"

"There's time before dinner."

"What kind of help is Myling's husband looking for?"

"It's none of your concern."

Raina glanced down at her shoes. He was right. She didn't want to get involved with his life or his business. "Myling doesn't look remotely jealous that you're with someone else."

Sonny's face became expressionless. "I'm over her."

"Ooookay." Raina dragged the word out. If he were over

her, then how come he didn't greet her? "So why am I here?"

"You're here so my grandfather doesn't set me up with someone," Sonny said. "I don't want to marry for an alliance."

"You don't strike me as someone who wants to marry for love." Actually, he didn't strike Raina as someone who would think about marriage. Didn't he have enough problems without a woman to further complicate his life?

"I don't want a marriage like my brother's. Lily's family controls the drug trade in Thailand. At first, it seemed the marriage might work, but then Jerry found out she is barren. Now they're stuck with each other."

"Why can't they get a divorce?"

"And sever the ties to the Nine Dragons' best supplier?" Sonny shrugged. "Not going to happen as long as my grandfather is alive."

"Is their childless situation the reason you became Dai Lo?"

Sonny studied her as if weighing her worth. In the end, he found her lacking. "Are you going to change your shoes?"

Raina held up the palms of her hands. "I'm trying to understand what's expected of me. What will you tell them...when this is over?"

He gave her a cheeky grin. "What if you want to stay engaged? There are advantages to being a Big Sister."

Since Dai Lo's literal translation meant big brother, his wife would naturally be a big sister in the criminal organization.

An image of diamonds and expensive clothes flashed through Raina's mind. But an orange jumpsuit hovered over the privileged life built on a foundation of dirty money. "Sorry, this isn't the life I want for me or my future children."

"Smart girl."

Raina glanced at the pile of gifts on the side table next to the staircase. Three wine glasses were clustered at the end of the table and the wine tray tipped against the wall to make room for the gifts. An old-fashioned desk clock sat like a cake topper in the middle of the pile. She gasped, pointing at the clock. "Where did that come from?"

Dread settled into her stomach. To give someone a clock meant the giver wished the recipient would die. And to give one as a birthday gift was extremely bad luck. This Chinese superstition had caused more than one multi-generational family feud in the old country. Who would want Kwan Gong to die?

Sonny marched over to the gifts and snatched up the clock. "Did you see who brought this?"

She shook her head. "It must have been concealed. Who would be stupid enough to walk in holding it?" Especially when half the guests were packing heat.

His knuckles whitened around the clock. "I have to get rid of this before anyone else sees it."

Raina watched Sonny march out of the foyer and past the ballroom. She took a deep breath, spooked by the clock, and Sonny's reaction to it. Superstition ran deep in many modern Chinese families, and a hidden enemy was baiting the Kwans.

3

THE WALKING DEAD

Raina swiped a glass of wine from the side table. She took a gulp of wine and smacked her lips at the faint berry taste. Yum. She trotted upstairs to change her shoes. Maybe she could even hide out in her room for a few minutes. Her purse buzzed, and by the ringtone, she knew it was her grandma. She sat down on the stone bench in the nearest alcove and pulled out her phone.

GOT A BACKUP LIFELINE. ON MY WAY

She took another gulp of wine. When her gaze returned to the phone, the message was still there. Why couldn't her grandmother follow directions? Her fingers flew across the screen on her phone.

STAY HOME. WE'RE IN THE LIMO—

Click!

Raina glanced up from the phone but didn't see anyone in the hallway. She returned to her text message.

—GOING TO A HOTEL BALLROOM—

Someone moaned. *Thud! Thud!*

Raina glanced up to see Jerry staggering toward her. Where did he come from?

Jerry kept his chin tucked against his chest. He moaned again, hunched over his stomach. He was less than a foot away from Raina, but he didn't seem to be aware of her. She opened her mouth to call out to him, but he gasped. A hoarse rattling sound that sent a chill down her spine and froze her on the spot. He fell to his knees beside her and sprawled across her lap before she could react.

Raina managed to save the wine, but the impact of Jerry's body falling on her lap knocked the phone out of her hands and the stuffing out of her. A toilet paper wad from her bra dropped onto the back of his neck. She blinked, but the crumpled white paper was still on the black hair. She used her index finger to nudge the side of his head, but he didn't move...or breathe.

Fudge.

She glanced around the small alcove in the east wing of the mansion but didn't see anything that could get her out of her current situation. It seemed rather callus to push him off her lap, but his dead weight pinned her lower body to the stone bench.

Her hand shook, but she slurped down the rest of the wine without spilling it on her dress. She didn't want a stain on her chest when she spoke to the police later. She had no doubt they would be joining the party before the end of the evening.

But first, she had to get away from Jerry before the henchmen showed up, or his wouldn't be the only dead body lying around. With the two factions of the Nine Dragons faking nice downstairs, Sonny would kill her himself for adding to his to-do list when he was already hustling to solidify his leadership.

Raina set the crystal flute down, re-padded the girls with the toilet paper, and took a deep rattling breath. She lifted her shaking hands, hovering them over Jerry's head. Her heart hammered against her chest.

"What the—"

Raina glanced up. "Sonny!" She sagged back against the wall behind her. "Get him off me." Her voice came out in an unfamiliar high pitch.

Sonny rushed over from the intersection where the main hall led to the east wing. He grabbed his brother's shoulder and shook him. "Jerry!" No answer. He turned his brother over, sliding him onto the floor.

Raina wiggled her toes, sharpening the pins and needles feeling. She hobbled into a standing position but held onto the wall in case she toppled over in her heels.

Sonny felt for a pulse on Jerry's neck. His brown eyes darkened, highlighting the silver scar on the side of his face. He glanced at Raina. "Did someone pay you to kill my brother?"

The blood rushed in Raina's ears, and she swayed. If Sonny, the Dai Lo of the Nine Dragons triad, turned on her, she was dead meat. She shook her head.

"I was texting my grandma...I heard a shuffle, and he fell on me, knocking my phone onto the floor." She pointed at the pieces of her phone on the floor. "He made a gurgling sound...went limp...I don't know what happened." Her breaths came out in short, noisy puffs. She refused to glance at Jerry's swollen face.

Sonny checked his brother's pockets and came up with a cell phone and wallet. He flipped through the wallet and put it back into Jerry's pocket. "Give me your purse."

Raina clutched the tiny evening bag in front of her. "Can I go home now? I don't want to be involved in this."

Sonny snatched the purse from her and tossed his brother's phone inside. He scooped up the pieces of her phone and also dumped it inside her handbag. He grabbed her hands, dragging her away from the intersection. "Too late, Rainy. Dinner is about to start. Let's go."

Raina trotted alongside him, her heels clicking on the floor, and the silk dress fluttering against her legs. "What about Jerry?"

"We'll talk later, but we can't be seen with his body. Neither of us would survive the fallout."

"But you're Dai Lo..."

"The other faction would love to use Jerry's death to get rid of me."

Raina stumbled and would have fallen if Sonny hadn't caught her. As his fake fiancée, she was also caught in the middle of the criminal organization's power struggle. And all because she wanted to get her deceased grandfather's journal back. Why didn't she say no when Sonny suggested the faked engagement?

Footsteps headed toward them from the staircase.

Raina couldn't breathe. *Oh, no...*

Sonny tugged her against a doorway. "Follow my lead." His tone was calm, and his eyes glittered with excitement. He was obviously enjoying the rush of adrenaline from the trap closing in on them. He ran his fingers through her chignon until the hairpins fell against the floor.

Raina grabbed the hair sticks. "What are you doing?" she whispered.

He buried one hand in her curly black hair and put the other on her hip. "Now wrap a leg around me."

She ignored his instruction. There was no way she could hold herself upright in these heels with only one foot on the ground.

He pressed his firm body against her, and she jumped at the bulge. She shouldn't be surprised he had a gun, but the reminder he wasn't one of the good guys wasn't something she needed at the moment. His lips crushed hers, and she stiffened.

"Relax," he mumbled against her mouth.

The footsteps came closer.

Raina flung her arms around him and kissed him like her life depended on it. His tongue traced her lower lip, and his scent—a light breezy aftershave with hints of his maleness—enveloped her. The fabric of his tuxedo brushed against her skin. Her legs wobbled with fear, and he tightened his grip on her.

She was going to die. They would take her outside and beat her for answers. They would pull out her fingernails and...

"Ahem," someone said.

Sonny slowly pulled away from her and caught her wide eyes. "They have silicone padding that is more natural, Rainy," he whispered. He leaned in to kiss her nose.

Raina blinked at his comment. What?

He turned to glare at Cat and another henchman. "What do you want?" The chill in his voice cooled Raina's blood.

The smirk left the henchman's face, but Cat continued to grin. The Hispanic woman was in head-to-toe tight black leather like she was heading to a bikers' convention. Totally inappropriate for the dinner party. Raina didn't even want to know where she hid her gun.

"Dai Lo, it's time for dinner," the henchman said.

"Kwan Gong asked us to find you," Cat said.

Sonny stepped in front of Raina, blocking her from the stares. With his broad shoulder as a shield, she straightened out her appearance. A wad of toilet paper peeked out from her bra. Her face burned, and she stuffed it back into her chest. She pulled the rest of her hair out of the chignon and tucked the hair sticks into her purse.

"Rainy, are you ready for dinner?" Sonny asked over his shoulder.

"Yes...yes. I'm starving," Raina mumbled.

The henchmen snickered. "I'll bet you are."

Cat slapped the man. *Crack!*

Raina flinched, and she grabbed Sonny's hand.

"Have more respect for the Dai Lo's fiancee. She's not a fu—"

"That's enough," Sonny snapped. "Go. We'll be there in a minute."

The henchmen turned toward the main hall, but Cat

paused, squinting at the corridor behind them. "Is there someone down there?"

Raina kept her gaze fixed on Sonny's shoulder blade to keep from whipping around to see if Jerry's legs stuck out from the alcove.

Sonny glanced casually behind him and turned back to Cat. "I'm going down for dinner. You can stay here if you want." He headed toward the main hall, tugging Raina along. The man had nerves of steel.

She trotted along, swinging her hips like a bimbolina. Sonny wanted a smart girl from a good family to play the role of his fiancée, but this was much easier. Everyone always underestimated a bimbolina.

Footsteps followed from a discreet distance behind them.

The area behind Raina's shoulder blade tingled as if waiting for a knife. The longer she kept up this charade, the further she would be sucked into this violent world. Sonny could have killed his brother to solidify his leadership in the Nine Dragons. But so could she. To everyone else in the ballroom, their future was linked.

Her heart rate slowed to normal by the time they joined the rest of the party. Several people glanced over at their entrance and returned to their conversations. Sonny nodded at the man by the dinner gong and headed toward the archway leading into the formal dining room.

Booong!

The dinner gong rang behind them, and the other guests proceeded toward the dining room. Raina ended up seated between Sonny and Freddie Low, the Dai Lo of the Black Tiger triad who married Sonny's ex-fiancée. Great.

He was in his early forties with neatly trimmed salt-and-pepper hair. His bespoke black tuxedo probably cost more than Raina's rent and his diamond cufflinks were certainly worth more than her annual income. He exuded wealth and power like his family had had it for generations.

"Congratulations on your engagement to Sonny Kwan," Freddie said in Chinese. "So what are you bringing into the marriage, Miss Sun?"

Raina pasted a smile on her face and willed her thoughts away from the dead body upstairs. She had to play it cool until someone else discovered the body. "Just my fabulous self. He fell in love with my brains."

Sonny gave her an encouraging look but returned to his conversation with the elderly woman on the other side of him.

Freddie raised an eyebrow. "Undoubtedly. I heard your mother is a Wong. As in Wong International Shipping. This is quite an alliance for Sonny. And your family will be helping with his...business?"

"No. They don't even know I'm engaged."

The woman next to Freddie leaned in to watch the two of them. Myling Low was in her late twenties and lovely—a mix of Filipino and Chinese descent—with a natural tan that Raina envied. Her hair, a thick black mane, was loose over her bare shoulders, and her full lips quirked in a knowing smile.

Nope, Sonny's ex wasn't even remotely jealous.

When Freddie turned away to whisper something to Myling, Raina let out a sigh of relief. The area between her shoulder blades ached from the tension. Any minute now, someone would burst into the dining room and point a finger at her.

Across from her, the empty seat next to Lily Kwan drew Raina's eyes like a beacon. Lily didn't seem concerned her husband wasn't at the table. Did Jerry blame his wife for the loss of the Dai Lo position to his younger brother? Why was her barrenness an issue? In the old days, it would signify Jerry's weakness, but this was the twenty-first century.

Yes, but their grandfather grew up in a remote village in China, said a small voice in Raina's mind.

From the corner of her eye, Raina peeked at Kwan Gong, the patriarch of the Kwan family, sitting at the head of the table. Gong was the formal title for maternal grandfather and also a term of respect for an elderly man. No one at the table would dare call him anything else.

He was a few years younger than her grandma, but he didn't have her vigor. Slightly stooped with a wan face, he could be recovering from a recent illness. Raina would have put him in bed instead of letting him hold court.

Kwan Gong frowned at the archway as if waiting for someone to appear. He didn't even know his eldest grandson was dead in the hallway upstairs.

Footsteps pounded outside the archway, the noise of a conversation, and a servant rushed into the dining room. He whispered into Kwan Gong's ear.

Raina's stomach fluttered. This was it. A ring of men would surround her any minute now to prevent her escape. Her breath became shallow, and she had to force herself to breathe normally.

Everyone continued eating and drinking, but Sonny

watched his grandfather from the corner of his eye. Kwan Gong said something to the servant, and the servant disappeared from the room.

Sonny squeezed her thigh underneath the table. He whispered into her ear, "Relax."

Raina folded her hands on her lap like a naughty child waiting for her punishment. Freddie glanced at her in puzzlement but returned to the conversation with his wife.

The same servant appeared in the archway again. A hand holding a pimp cane with a golden horse statuette pushed him aside. And Po Po stepped into view in a metallic-magenta ball gown with cone-shaped breasts and linebacker shoulder pads. Her silver hair was held back by a scrunchie and hair sticks. It looked like Raina's lifeline had transformed into an anchor.

4

THE PARTY POOPER

P o Po swaggered over to Kwan Gong, and he got up to kiss her hand. They chatted while the servant pulled a chair up to the table. Several people stood while the servant made room for the extra place setting.

Raina gave herself a mental head slap. Of course, her grandma would have known Kwan Gong. Her husband had saved his life and later helped him immigrate to the United States. How come her grandma didn't use her connection to get her husband's journal back? Sometimes Raina hated the secretive nature of Chinese families for hiding dirty laundry.

Po Po sat in the chair the servant held out to her. When she turned to hook her cane on the back of the chair, the man next to her jerked back. The linebacker shoulder pads missed his eyes by a mere inch.

"What's up with the dress?" Sonny asked. "It looks like a bad prom dress."

Raina ignored his comment, and he resumed his conversation with the elderly woman next to him.

Conversations resumed and food platters sailed out at regular intervals from the kitchen. The crystal flutes winked in the dim lighting. Silver forks scraped against the fine china. If Raina squinted, she could forget about the dead body upstairs.

She glanced at the empty spot next to Lily. Wasn't anyone concerned Jerry was MIA?

The man sitting next to Po Po burst into a full belly laugh. Her grandma said something Raina couldn't hear, but if she had to guess, it would be "do too" like a kinder-gartener wanting to prove herself on the playground.

Po Po grabbed her cane, and her fingers hovered dangerously over the balls of the horse statuette. If her grandma pressed the trigger, a spray of skunk oil would drench her dinner companion.

Raina tapped Sonny's hand to get his attention. "Why don't you toast your grandfather's health, honey?"

Sonny gave her a quizzical look but stood, using his fork to tap on his wineglass.

Tink. Tink. Tink.

Conversation ceased. Po Po glanced over like everyone else.

Raina took a deep breath. Disaster averted.

"I want to toast—" Sonny's voice trailed off as the commotion outside echoed into the dining room. He glanced at the archway.

Raina followed his gaze. An ashen servant rushed in, wringing his hands. *Oh, no...*

Sonny set his glass on the table and strolled over to the servant.

34

"Mr. Kwan...Mr. Kwan is dead," the servant babbled to Sonny.

The room became eerily silent.

Sonny grabbed the servant's arm and hauled him out of the room. Cat got up to follow them.

Freddie whispered to Myling, "I would beat him before firing him. What an unlucky thing to say."

The room grew stuffy. The guests looked at each other with wide eyes, and the whispering began.

Raina rose, tapping on her glass. "Let me finish what Sonny was about to say," she said in Chinese. "Kwan Gong, may you live for another hundred years. And may it be filled with your family gathered under one roof." She fell back to the traditional blessings.

Kwan Gong's scowl melted. "And may you give me great-grandsons, dear girl." He chuckled and broke the tension in the room.

Raina dropped to her chair, her face hot. No, no...this was meant to be a weekend gig.

They were in the middle of eating the birthday cake when Cat came back. She whispered something to Kwan Gong, and the two of them left the room. This was no way to celebrate a seventieth birthday party.

As the only remaining family member, Lily led the guests into the ballroom where a band played a lively jazz tune. The guests drifted into small groups, and a few couples danced.

When Po Po led her dinner partner toward the dance floor, Raina snagged her grandma's arm. "We need to talk."

"What?" Po Po asked, forcing a smile onto her face. "I'm busy, and I don't have time for a lecture."

Her dinner partner glanced away to give them the facade of privacy.

Raina waved him off. "Her dance card is full for the evening." She dragged her grandma to a quieter part of the room. "What are you doing here? Didn't we agree for you to wait by the phone?"

"And miss all this?" Po Po waved at the dancing couples and the buffet of desserts and drinks. "No, it's not fair you get to have all the fun."

Raina stared at her grandma in disbelief. "I wouldn't call having a dead body on your lap fun." She filled her grandma in on Jerry's death. "His supporters would have a field day with me if they knew what happened. I'm not sure if Sonny could protect me when push comes to shove."

As Po Po listened to Raina's tale, her eyes grew wider. "You're kidding me, right? Couldn't you jump out of the way?"

"It was the strangest thing. One second the hall was empty, and the next he was on my lap. He appeared out of nowhere."

"Maybe he stumbled out of a secret chamber," Po Po said.

The mansion was old enough to have hidden servant halls. "Are you thinking Nancy Drew or Harry Potter?"

Her grandma's eyes gleamed. "Does it matter? We're hot on the trail of another murder. It's so much fun having you around."

Raina shook her head "Oh, no. We're here for the journal. I get through the police interview, and I've done my part of the bargain."

"We have to help my old friend, Kwan Gong."

"Old friend? A few months ago you didn't even recall his name."

Po Po waved dismissively. "Small details. What matters now is that we're here to help."

"You're just bored."

"You would be bored too if you had to sit in the rental all day long. There's only so many times I can walk around the block."

"I told you not to come to Toronto with me."

Her grandmother ignored the comment. "How did Jerry die?"

Raina shivered at the memory of the swollen face. "I think he was poisoned. I didn't see any wounds. And his face was... I don't understand why Sonny left his brother in the hall though. You would think he'd call for an ambulance."

"Was Jerry already dead when he got there?"

"Yes."

"Sonny probably didn't want to be found next to his brother's body. With things the way they are, he had the most to gain from his brother's death."

Raina nodded. "And as his fiancée, so do I."

Cat appeared at the entrance of the ballroom, her eyes scanning the guests. Her eyes locked in on Raina, and she crooked a finger.

Raina took a deep breath to steady herself. "It looks like the jig is up."

AS THEY APPROACHED THE LIBRARY, Raina heard Kwan Gong's raspy voice before she saw him.

"This is all your fault, Sonny," Kwan Gong said. "If you had let your brother continue as the figurehead for the Nine Dragons, he wouldn't be dead." His voice broke in the end.

"We both know he's too weak to do what needs to be done. You think I want to be Dai Lo? When I already have a taste for freedom?" Sonny's voice sounded bitter. "I'm not repeating my father's mistakes."

"If I'd known you would turn out like this, I would have drowned you in the toilet."

Raina gasped. *Ouch!*

Po Po leaned over to whisper in Raina's ear. "I've said worse to my boys."

Cat stepped aside, and Raina got a good look at the library for the first time. Kwan Gong and Sonny scowled at each other across a mahogany desk. Even with the differences in their age, she could see the family resemblance in their profiles—the same full lips and sharp nose.

However, Kwan Gong's pale face highlighted his wrinkles and sunspots, while Sonny's more youthful face blazed with a quiet power that threatened violence even in this domestic setting. They glanced over when Raina and Po Po stepped into the room.

Raina's smile wobbled. She didn't want to get involved in someone else's family drama. Hers was bad enough. She glanced around the traditional library. Dark wooden shelves and new leather-covered books. The two reading chairs were grouped in front of the fireplace. It didn't look as if they were planning to interrogate her. Maybe she could leave with her grandma in one piece.

"Ah, here's your beautiful fiancée," Kwan Gong said,

attempting to smile, or at least the loose skin under his jaw wobbled. "And her lovely grandma. How was your dinner, Bonnie?"

Po Po sniffed. "The chicken was too dry."

This time Kwan Gong's lips curled into a real smile. "Looks like you still have the knack for showing up at the perfect time. Getting engaged to your granddaughter seems to be the only thing Sonny got right."

"Is something wrong?" Po Po asked as if Raina hadn't briefed her on the situation in the ballroom.

"My eldest grandson..." Kwan Gong paused and swallowed. "Died. The lazy lout died on my birthday."

"I'm sorry," Po Po said, lowering her voice until it was almost a whisper. "Is there anything we can do to help?"

Kwan Gong nodded, accepting the words stiffly. "There's no time to grieve. We need damage control. I don't want the police questioning the triad elders and Freddie Low."

"I don't see how it can be avoided," Raina said. "The police will question everyone when they get here."

Sonny glanced at his grandfather from the corner of his eye.

Raina's lips tightened. They didn't call the police yet? "Did you at least cover him with a sheet?" As soon as the words left her mouth, she regretted her tone.

"Yes, we did," Sonny said, giving her a significant look. "I'm surprised he didn't just fall on someone's lap."

Raina averted her gaze. Right, this was the first time she heard of Jerry's death. She should let them figure out how to handle this, and she had a feeling he was protecting her from the internal politics.

Kwan Gong narrowed his eyes at her. "Did I miss something?"

The mood in the room dropped further into the arctic zone. Sonny stiffened, but he kept silent. Cat's hand drifted to her shoulder harness while her eyes watched Raina like she was a dangerous animal.

Raina's stomach did a backflip. What if Kwan Gong thought she had something to do with Jerry's death? "There's no rat here," she addressed the henchwoman, trying to buy herself time.

Cat flushed. Her hand drifted back to her side, but her stony expression was anything but relaxed.

Raina glanced at Kwan Gong. "In the States, we call the police when there's a death. Isn't it the same here? Or do you have to call a doctor?" She widened her eyes in pretend shock as if she had a sudden thought. "Do you suspect foul play?"

Po Po gasped, her hands flying to cover her mouth. "You mean we had dinner with a murderer?" Her eyes rolled to the back of her head, and she would have fallen if Cat hadn't caught her.

The henchwoman lowered Po Po to the ground and checked her pulse. "It's steady. The news must have shocked the old bird."

Raina suppressed the urge to roll her eyes. What a drama queen. She glanced at the concerned faces. At least her grandma broke the tension in the room.

"Don't let her lie on the ground. Get her on the sofa," Kwan Gong said, pointing to the sofa under the window.

Cat scooped the tiny grandma up and carried her over. Kwan Gong directed the henchwoman on how to make Po Po more comfortable.

"Whoever killed my brother is dancing downstairs and sipping my champagne," Sonny whispered into Raina's ear.

"The thought has crossed my mind," Raina said. "We'll leave you to figure things out then. It looks like my grandma is waking up."

Po Po pressed the back of her hand to her forehead, moaning. "What...what happened?"

Kwan Gong spoke quietly to her grandma.

Sonny turned away from the theatrics at the sofa. "I need you to talk to the women downstairs. See if they noticed anything before Jerry's death. They'll clam up if Cat or I do it. I don't know if Lily will be up to the task once she finds out her husband is dead."

"She doesn't know?" Raina asked.

"You see her here?"

"But—"

"She's a wild card. I don't know how she'll react to the news. With the triad elders downstairs, we can't have her make a scene."

Raina frowned. *So it's better to keep the wife in the dark? Geez...* "I'm not a trained investigator. You should leave this to the police."

"You have the people skills and instincts for this. I've seen how you solved the murder in San Francisco. Do we have a deal?" Sonny raised an eyebrow. "For your grandfather's journal?"

Raina glanced at her grandma sitting up on the sofa. Did she have a choice? They needed the journal, and he had it. Her hands curled into fists. It was one thing to pretend to be a fiancée, but another to get involved in a murder investigation. She wasn't sure her curiosity would let her stop at asking a few questions.

"You can't just change the terms of our original deal. Where's your fu—" She broke off and swallowed. She needed to calm down. She forced her hands to relax. "Where's your honor? How do you expect me to trust you?"

"I'm sorry, but I need help, and you're here." He sounded like the circumstances forced his hand. "If I had a choice, I wouldn't want you to get involved in this."

She scowled at him. What could she do to shift the power in this relationship so he didn't hold all the cards? Would talking to his family and associates turn up something she could use to her advantage? "How do I know you still have the journal?"

Sonny flashed her a roguish smile. "You'll have to trust me."

"Sure, I trust you. Now let's verify it."

Sonny chuckled. He leaned in until she could smell him. A light breezy aftershave that reminded her of the ocean. "I'll give you a hint. Your grandfather went to China specifically to seek this woman whom he later married."

Raina's eyes widened with excitement. He'd read the journal! "What do you mean? My grandfather went to China in 1962 to help with the Great Leap Forward policies to gain his father's approval."

"That was the cover story."

"I don't understand. Was this woman an old girlfriend?"

"No, he never met her before."

Now Raina was more confused than ever. She'd

assumed Ah Gong fell in love with someone else while he was engaged to Po Po, but honored the engagement anyway. During that time period in the old country, an engaged woman was as good as married. For Ah Gong to not go through with the marriage would have meant Po Po would be ostracized and shamed among her family and friends.

Sonny gave her a bemused look. "Help me, and I'll help you."

Raina narrowed her eyes so he wouldn't think he'd won her cooperation so easily. "No games. I need to know what happened in China."

He nodded. "You can trust me."

Uh-huh, Raina thought.

"What are you two lovebirds whispering about?" Po Po called out from the sofa.

Kwan Gong and Cat turned to watch the two of them.

Raina's mind whirled with what Sonny had told her. She tried to step away from him, but he wrapped an arm around the small of her back and pulled her up against him.

"Just making plans for later," Sonny said.

Kwan Gong harrumphed, frowning at his remaining grandson. "Get a move on it, and find out what you can. I need to call the police." At Sonny's raised eyebrow, he said, "It's not like we can dump Jerry's body in a lake. You probably have a good hour before they show up to question everyone about the murder."

"What makes you so sure it's murder?" Po Po asked.

"In our profession, it's always murder," Kwan Gong said. "But we take care of our own."

Raina shivered at the chill in his voice. She believed

in justice, but not the eye for an eye code of honor among men like the Kwans. Sonny's arm tightened around her. His body heat seeped through the thin silk and warmed her side, but did nothing to warm the cold brick on her chest.

Not only did she have to find the murderer and get the journal back, but she also must turn this person over to the police before the Nine Dragons avenged Jerry's death. She glanced at Po Po tapping her pimp cane impatiently on the carpet floor. And keep her grandma safe. Easy peasy.

5

BUILDING A MOUSETRAP

R aina closed the door to the library and headed toward the ballroom. Sonny, his grandfather, and Cat remained behind to plan for the police's arrival. They probably had to figure out how to hide the Nine Dragons' criminal activities from the police.

"Good job on the fainting," Raina said.

Po Po smirked, pleased with herself. "That was an award-winning performance. My mother would have been proud of me."

Raina didn't know what to think of Po Po's fondness for her mother. Tai Po had abandoned Po Po to the other wives when she fell out of favor with her husband, the wealthy rice merchant who rescued her from the stage. Being the third wife who only gave birth to a girl in the old country couldn't have been easy.

She filled her grandma in on her modified bargain with Sonny but left out what he'd revealed about Ah Gong purposely seeking the other woman. This detail was a game changer, but she wasn't sure it was for the better. And there was no point in worrying her grandma about this until she knew more.

The smile left her grandmother's face. "Rainy, you can walk away from this anytime you want."

"What about you? Can you walk away from this?"

"No. I have to know why my husband cheated on me. It's a lodestone that will steal my joy for life." Her grandmother's eyes gleamed with determination. "I'm even willing to use my wiles to lure Kwan Gong into bed for pillow talk."

Raina covered her ears with her hands. "La-la-la. I don't need to hear about your bedroom gymnastics. I thought you're supposed to be a role model for me."

"How am I not a good role model? Am I not teaching you to speak up and love yourself?" Po Po winked. "You don't know how hard it is to find a man my age who can keep up with me. The little blue pill can only last so long before it runs out of juice. Sometimes I think I'm better off with a battery."

A snort came from behind them. Raina glanced back to find Cat breathing down their necks. The woman moved like a ninja. How much of the conversation had she overheard?

"Excuse me, ladies," Cat said and passed them in the hallway.

Raina scowled at her back and waited until the henchwoman was out of hearing distance to whisper to her grandma. "How deep is her loyalty to Sonny?"

"Why do you care?" Po Po asked.

"Would she kill Jerry to help stabilize Sonny's regime?"

"With or without Sonny's approval?"

Raina gave Po Po a sideways glance. Her grandma was a lot more perceptive than her outward appearance led someone to believe. "Do you think Sonny would put out the hit on his own brother?"

Po Po shrugged. "Hard to say. Divided loyalties are never a good thing, especially for an organization like the Nine Dragons. And I've seen worse in families who fight over less."

They turned a corner and approached the opened double doors leading into the ballroom. The lights were dim, and soft music floated out toward them. Raina popped her head into the ballroom and scanned the crowd. Lily was nowhere in sight. Myling and Freddie danced cheek to cheek.

Raina turned to her grandma. "Let's go find the kitchen. Lily Kwan might be in there. Besides, I want to check the place out before the police secure it. Do you think someone put the poison in the food or drink?"

"The staff will be on top of each other, preparing the food and serving the dishes. It's possible they won't notice an extra person in the kitchen, but if you were the killer, would you risk it?"

Raina shook her head. "I wouldn't want the staff describing me to the police. If it's poison, the killer could slip it into the food or drink after it left the kitchen. But this meant the killer would practically have to be next to Jerry to get it into his food or drink or risk killing somebody else by accident."

They passed the ballroom and kept going to the end of the hall. They turned left—to a dead end.

Raina stared at the wall with hands on her hips. "Didn't the food come from this direction?"

Po Po stepped closer to the wallpaper and walked along it. Her hand reached out and twisted a knob. A panel swung smoothly open, inches from her face. "Open sesame. A servant door."

Raina peered down at the steps leading to another floor below. A "downstairs" world like a *Downton Abbey* episode. The sound of clattering utensils and pots and the low hum of conversation drifted toward them.

Po Po elbowed her way in front of Raina and started down the stairs, her ruffles swooshing with each step. "You coming?" she called out over her shoulder.

Raina followed her grandma, her heel tapping at the wood steps. If she didn't change shoes soon, she would end up with blisters.

The stairs ended at a dim and narrow hallway. A few steps to the right, light spilled out from a bustling kitchen. A door clicked closed further down the hall. Raina squinted. Did the slim back belong to Cat?

Po Po strolled into the kitchen like she belonged there. Raina hurried after her grandma.

A woman in a head-to-toe black outfit set down her serving tray and hurried over. "Can I help you?" The rest of the staff glanced up and returned to their tasks.

While Po Po chattered about the soup they had had over dinner, Raina scanned the area. Her grandmother was right. Too many pairs of eyes watched them. What if the killer was someone the staff recognized?

A flash of gold caught the corner of Raina's eye. She took a step back into the hall and glanced up in time to see Lily heading upstairs. Since she was the lady of the mansion, she had every right to be here. Except, why was she skulking in the other rooms?

"Lily," Raina called out and hurried after her.

Lily Kwan hesitated, and turned toward Raina, her hand gripping the rail. "Yes?" While her tone was friendly enough, her body language said she couldn't get away fast enough.

Without her husband towering next to her, Lily Kwan's beauty looked less fragile than she first appeared. Her diamond shaped face was freckled with a wholesome luminous quality like she never had a stressful day in her life. Since Raina knew this wasn't true, she figured Lily must have expensive makeup.

A door clicked open from behind them. Raina whipped around to see Cat coming out of the second door past the kitchen. She held a Louis Vuitton overnight bag, and her eyes flickered from Lily to Raina. Her purposeful strides slowed to a crawl. The wary expression on Cat's face seemed out of context with the situation. Was she worried Raina would tell Lily about her husband's death?

"Did you need something, Raina?" Lily asked, avoiding eye contact with Cat.

"Kwan Gong is looking for you. He's in the library," Raina said, studying Lily and Cat. Why was the henchwoman holding an overnight bag? If she were meant to be a guest, wouldn't she have been assigned a bedroom like Raina was upon arrival?

"Okay, thanks." Lily's words came out in a rush. She hurried upstairs without a backward glance.

By this time, Cat was at the foot of the stairs. She gave

Raina a wide berth, brushing the walls with her shoulders.

"Are we expecting more overnight guests?" Raina asked, nodding at the bag. "Seems like a wasted effort to bring the bag up from the car when she'll decline the invitation when the police show up." And why would the second-in-command for the Nine Dragons carry the bag when there were plenty of servants to do the work?

"Kwan Gong wasn't looking for Lily," Cat said, ignoring the question.

"It seemed cruel to have her find out about her husband's death at the same time as everyone else."

"Sonny told you specifically to talk to the women in the ballroom. What are you doing down here?"

"I could ask you the same question," Raina said.

"The cook wouldn't give me—" Po Po stepped into the narrow hallway. Her gaze flickered from Raina to Cat. "What's going on here?"

"Just reminding your granddaughter to take care of business." Cat headed upstairs, her hands tightening on the handle of the overnight bag.

"Who wears tight leather like that to a dinner party?" Po Po asked loudly so Cat could hear the comment. The henchwoman slammed the panel shut above them.

Raina marched to the door Cat had emerged from, grabbed the knob, and twisted. Locked.

"Let me try. Where is your hair stick?" Po Po said, holding out her hand.

Raina dug in her purse—her fingers brushed against sharp plastic—and handed one hair stick to Po Po. Her broken cell phone reminded Raina she also had a dead man's cell phone in her purse. What if the police searched everyone's bags?

A bead of sweat rolled down the small of her back. Wiping off her fingerprints and leaving the cell phone somewhere would be the smart thing to do. Why did Sonny take his brother's cell phone from the crime scene? What if fragments of her broken cell phone in the alcove pointed the finger back to her?

The servant her grandma spoke to earlier sailed out of the kitchen with a platter filled with finger foods. She glanced over and hesitated.

Raina stepped in front of her grandma and made a shooing motion with her hands. The servant shrugged and headed upstairs.

The latchkey clicked open behind her. "Open sesame," Po Po said, pride filling her voice.

Raina slipped into the room after her grandma and closed the door. She wasn't sure what to expect, but a windowless storage room of odds and ends wasn't it.

Her gaze swept over the piles of discarded linens, broken chairs at various stages of repair, and other flea market quality junk. The Louis Vuitton bag that Cat was holding would have stood out like a sparkling diamond in this crowd. What was it doing down here in the first place?

Po Po scowled at the junk. "Are you kidding me? I wasted my talent on this? There better be a dead body in here somewhere." She picked her way between the various piles until she was in the middle of the room. "Nope, nothing interesting here."

Raina turned to face the door. A glint of gold caught her eye next to the doorframe. She picked up the gold bead and held it up against the overhead light. It was from Lily Kwan's dress.

"I think Cat's bag came from this room," Raina said.

"A bag like that wouldn't last a minute in this junk room. A servant would have claimed it," Po Po said.

"My thought exactly." Raina explained her suspicion about Cat and Lily meeting here a few minutes before their encounter in the hallway. "Why are they meeting in secret so shortly after her husband's death?"

"Maybe they're having an affair?" Po Po's eyes lit up. "And they packed a getaway bag to run off into the sunset together during the party."

"This isn't *Days of Our Lives*. And if they are planning to run off together, why did Cat bring the bag back upstairs?"

"Would you disappear after Jerry's death? It would look too suspicious. And they can't leave the bag down here when the police comb the place. No, they have to get the bag back upstairs into Lily's room."

"So you think the two of them killed Jerry? If Lily wanted to get rid of Jerry, she had plenty of opportunities to do it before now. And this murder is premeditated. Your average killer doesn't walk around with poison in their pockets," Raina said.

"But Lily's bad marriage is motive enough." Po Po frowned, considering her theories. "Or Cat could have killed Jerry for Lily so they didn't have to run off together."

"You're still basing this on the assumption that Cat and Lily are having an affair. We don't even know there's any truth to this."

"Let's go find out. I sure would like to put the squeeze on Cat. I want to make her squeal."

Raina shook her head. "I need to figure out what to do with Jerry's cell phone first. I can't let the police find me with this." She explained how it got into her purse. She pulled up the call history and text messages. "Strange. He'd texted a phone number with the name of 'Mis' five minutes before his death."

"What did it say?" Po Po asked, squinting at the display screen.

"Meet me at our spot. Ten minutes. Or our secret will no longer be a secret," Raina read out loud.

Po Po's eyes widened. "Whoa! Sounds like blackmail."

Raina scrolled through Jerry's browsing history. Nothing unusual there. "Everything in the phone looks normal. His previous texts to Mis are sexually explicit. I need to bleach my eyes after this."

Po Po held out her hand. "Let me see."

Raina cradled the phone close to her chest. "No. You're bad enough already without needing to read this stuff."

Her grandma harrumphed, folding her arms across her chest. "It's not fair you get to be Sherlock and have all the fun."

Raina ignored her grandma's comment. She wouldn't call being responsible fun. "If this person is the killer, he or she believes Jerry is dead. Now what would happen if Jerry texted this person back for another meeting?" she said as the plan formed in her mind.

Po Po reached out and patted Raina's cheek. "Now that's my smart girl. The killer will have to come and finish the job."

6

THE STOLEN CHEESE

They clattered up the stairs and through the servant door to an emptied hall. Outside the ballroom, Raina pulled out Jerry's cell phone. The tail end of an eighties song drifted out. Using her grandma's back as a shield, Raina resent the message to the phone number and slipped the phone back into her purse.

"We'll look suspicious standing here," she said, scanning the area for cover.

Other than a stone bench and two large potted plants, the area was bare. They couldn't even pretend to be taking a smoking break.

"Give me your shoe," Po Po said, holding out her hand.

Raina slipped off her shoe and handed it to her grandma. "What—"

Po Po slammed the heel against the stone bench.

Bam! Bam!

The heel dangled from the shoe.

"Now sit on the bench, and we'll fix your shoe," Po Po said.

Raina sat, and her grandma knelt next to her foot. She squirmed on the bench, uncomfortable with grandma tending to her like this.

"Will you stop wiggling around?" Po Po complained.

"You're my elder, and I have you massaging my feet. This doesn't feel right."

"We're acting, Rainy. If it'll make you feel better, you can give me a back rub later. Can you see the entrance to the ballroom?"

"You'll need to shift to the right. The shoulder pads are in the way. Where did you get this dress?"

"It's your sister's prom dress. I packed it just in case I needed something fancy."

Raina burst out laughing. Not only did the shoulder pads look like football padding, but the full skirt had enough ruffles to make her grandma walk sideways through a door. So this was the height of fashion when her big sister was in her teens. This was real prime. Cassie always looked so chic and put together.

A shuffling noise broke Raina's laughter. She rubbed her ankle as if she had twisted it when the heel broke off. With her head down, she peered at Lily coming out of the ballroom with a slight frown on her face. Either Lily hadn't chatted with Kwan Gong or she didn't care her husband died.

But if Mis was Lily, why didn't Jerry program his wife's name in his phone? Raina had assumed the phone number belonged to a mistress or someone even more unsavory.

Wait! Someone else was coming out.

Myling strode out of the ballroom. Her eyes shifted from Lily to Raina and her grandma on the bench. Half a second later, her husband joined her. Freddie whispered something into Myling's ear, and she giggled before playfully swatting him on the chest.

Footsteps approached from the foyer. And within seconds, Cat appeared, holding four bottles of wine. She paused, glancing at the small crowd, and marched inside the ballroom.

"Let's resend the text message again and see which one of them reaches for a cell phone," Po Po whispered.

"Too risky," Raina said. "I should probably have a chat with these women like I promised Sonny."

Lily pulled out a cell phone from her purse. She tapped on the screen and held the phone against her ear.

Raina's eyes widened. What if—

Her purse vibrated and buzzed.

Oh, no!

Raina grabbed her purse and met her grandma's wide eyes. She shook her head. Her grandma's solution to an awkward situation would be deadly in a windowless space. She reached for the cane, but her grandma's fingers were faster, jerking at the trigger on the horse statuette.

The lower jaw on the horse slid open and a squirt of pale yellow liquid arched through the air. The liquid splattered onto the Oriental rug in front of them. An oily rancid funk blossomed around them.

Raina gagged and tried breathing through her mouth, but the skunk oil filled her sinuses until she was blinking back the tears in her eyes. She grabbed her broken shoe and hobbled away from her grandma.

Lily's head swiveled up from her cell phone. Her beautiful face contorted into a thin-lipped grimace and flared nostrils.

"Sorry," Po Po said, pretending to be sheepish. Her eyes glittered with amusement. "It was the shark fin soup. If I'd known the cook used real shark fin instead of imitation, I wouldn't have tried it. The wasteful practice of cutting one part of an animal for soup just doesn't sit well with my stomach."

Lily wrinkled her nose and stalked back inside the ballroom, offended with Po Po's judgment on her menu. Myling and Freddie glided toward the foyer, avoiding eye contact like they didn't want to embarrass Po Po.

Raina took off her other shoe and padded barefoot after Lily. The skunk oil was quick thinking on her grandma's part, but this incident might end the party before the police got here.

Po Po followed her with a wide grin on her face. "Who's still got the superpower to clear a room faster than a speeding bullet?"

"I'm surprised you're not throwing up from the smell," Raina said.

"I'm immune to the smell," Po Po said. "Lost it after the first explosion in the kitchen."

"I think you ruined the rug."

"Collateral damage. It's to be expected in an investigation."

Raina made her way toward the opened French doors on the opposite wall of the ballroom entrance. She had lost her grandma along the way, but she wasn't worried. As the warm breeze lifted tendrils of her hair, she glanced around.

Cat and Lily discussed heavy business next to the punch bowl. Cat uncorked the wine while Lily ladled the punch into cups. There was something going on between the two of them, but Raina doubted it was an affair. Even though Cat was second-in-command after Sonny in the organization, it would be an unforgivable act to dally with Jerry's wife. Heck, by the way they were scowling at each other, they probably weren't even friends.

Raina made her way to the punch table, still carrying her shoes in her hands.

Cat took one look at Raina and strolled off without another word. Lily glared after the henchwoman, looking as if she didn't like how the conversation ended.

Raina sidled up to Lily and said, "So what time do these parties usually end? I hope it's not an all-nighter. I don't have the stamina to party like that anymore."

Even though she was barely over five feet, Lily somehow stared down at Raina. The thin eyebrows thickened by makeup were running from the stifling heat in the room. A chink in the armor? Time to turn up the heat even more.

Lily returned to filling the cups. "You better get used to it."

"How do you like being married into the family?"

"I'm married to the hired help."

"I'm not sure what you mean. Jerry is the eldest son."

Lily cut her eyes back at Raina. "Why are you rubbing salt into the wound?"

Raina blinked, not sure about what to say. She could sense animosity rolling off the woman, but she didn't know if it had to do with her sad marriage, Jerry's death, or Raina's engagement to Sonny. "I'm sorry. If you're so unhappy, couldn't Jerry get another...job?"

"Once you're in the triad, you're in for life. Just like you'll be trapped once you say 'I do.'" Lily paused, considering her words. "Actually it might be too late for you already."

Raina shivered, gooseflesh rising on her arms, her mouth dry as she thought of Jerry lying upstairs while everyone continued to party down here. "Did you talk to Kwan Gong?"

Lily shook her head. "I can't find him. And I have no idea where Jerry is. It's just like him to disappear. He's the one who wanted this stupid party."

The noise level at the entrance of the ballroom grew louder. People shuffled out of the way. The lights snapped on, and the music drew to a halt. The police had arrived.

THE POLICE SEPARATED the family members from the other guests in the ballroom. The crowd hummed with speculation thicker than the flies on rancid meat. A man claimed there was a burglary, but the woman next to him claimed there was a bomb threat.

After a police officer took down Raina's name and her relationship with the family, he told her to go to the library to await further questioning. She padded barefoot out of the ballroom, passing half a dozen police officers on the way. There were probably plenty more upstairs.

Another officer stood guard by the doorway of the library. Lily cried at one corner of the sofa while Kwan Gong looked on at the other. When Raina sat down next to Lily, the officer gestured for them to separate. Raina headed toward one of the reading chairs by the fireplace. Since Po Po wasn't in the room, Raina assumed her grandmother wasn't considered part of the family.

Raina closed her eyes and slouched on the chair. It was close to midnight, and from her previous experience with giving statements, it would be a few more hours yet before she could go to bed. She must have drifted off because the next thing she knew Sonny was draping his tuxedo jacket over her.

She blinked sleepily. "Is it my turn yet? Have you seen my grandmother?"

"Sorry, but the police will interview the family last. They want to get through the guests first so they can go home."

Raina reached to pull the jacket closer, jiggling her purse. She frowned. Why did it feel lighter? "I'm surprised you're allowed to talk to me. Aren't they afraid we will corroborate our stories?"

She opened her purse underneath the jacket and brushed her fingers around it—lipstick, hair sticks, wallet, and her broken phone. Someone had removed Jerry's cell phone.

Sonny tipped his chin at the officer watching them. "I told them you were cold. Don't worry, everything is under control. You'll be fine if you tell them the truth. It's not like you found the body." He gave her a significant look, waiting until she tipped her chin at him to show her understanding of the situation.

He shifted the other reading chair so he could see the police officer without turning his head. He flopped down on the chair and closed his eyes.

She studied him for a few seconds longer, but he ignored her. To all outward appearance, he looked as if he'd fallen asleep, but he didn't fool her. Given the family business, there was no way he could relax with the police crawling around his home.

He must have removed Jerry's cell phone when he draped the jacket over her. Why did he want her to lie to the police? Was it to protect her or to protect himself? Forensics would determine Jerry's time of death, so even if she fudged the truth, it wouldn't throw off the case. Should she go along with his plans?

Sonny cracked open an eyelid. "Relax. I can hear your brain cranking even from here."

"Easy for you to say. You know which side of the law you're on," Raina said, glancing at the police officer that appeared to be holding a conversation with someone in the hallway. "Did you kill Jerry?"

"Always going straight to the point. I could fall in love with a woman like you."

"Sorry, I'm already in love with another man." As soon as the words left her mouth, Raina wondered why she said it. It was none of his business, and she wasn't sure if it still counted after she rejected Matthew's proposal.

"You say it with such conviction." His tone was dismissive.

Right. Like you're over Myling, Raina thought. There was no point in pushing a hot button at a time like this. "It must be convenient now that your brother is dead."

"Convenient, yes, but not something I wanted. There are differing factions within the Nine Dragons, but we agreed only I have the strength to do what must be done."

"You didn't answer my question."

"I have nothing to do with my brother's death, but the triad elders would love to pin it on me."

"I don't understand. The elders are opposed to your leadership...why?"

"They're afraid of change. There's no need to bloody our hands to make money anymore. No one knows how many millions are siphoned from the US economy each year with just a few clicks of the mouse. It's much easier to commit a 'white-collar crime,' and with the right lawyer, the penalties are nothing compared to our bread-and-butter—drugs and firearms distribution."

"Ah, I see." And she did. He was still a criminal, but a smart one. "Jerry is the eldest. Couldn't he transform the Nine Dragons to a white-collar criminal organization?"

"He wasn't strong enough to stand up to the elders. And since he liked to sample the wares, you couldn't trust his judgment. He abdicated the leadership position when my grandfather had to take 'an early retirement.'"

Raina gave him a sideways glance. Early retirement? Or an internal coup to knock his grandfather off his position? She wasn't surprised Jerry was a drug addict. "Do you have Kwan Gong's support?"

Sonny shook his head. "He's the ringleader for the elders."

"I thought he retired."

"I might have the official leadership, but my grandfather still holds sway over many members of the organization. He got his power through the old-fashioned way. I'm not opposed to violence, but not as a first resort. I prefer to keep the blood off my designer clothes." He gave her a half smile, flashing the silver scar on the side of his face. "I'm a bit of a prima donna."

Raina snorted. An attractive criminal with a sense of humor. "How do I know you still have my grandfather's journal? The information in there threatens your precarious position as Dai Lo."

"I've already gotten rid of the sections that mentioned my grandfather. It's sweet you're worried about me, Rainy." His voice became a purr.

She tilted her head, giving him her best wide-eyed blink. "I can't seem to wrap my head around why my grandfather had a secret family. I know he loved my grandmother. You can't fake love for fifty years."

Sonny wagged his index finger at her. "Na-ah-ah. Not until you help me out with the women in this investigation. Did you talk to Lily or Myling?"

Raina shook her head. "Not until you can prove I'll get the journal back at the end of the investigation. You won't fool me again."

He shrugged casually. "You need to have faith that I have your best interest at heart."

"By lying to the police?"

"By keeping Jerry's supporters away from you. You might be my fiancée, but Jerry's father-in-law is the biggest drug lord in Thailand. His reach is long."

"I thought Jerry and Lily had a horrible marriage. Why would the father-in-law care?"

"Saving face is more important than his daughter's happiness. Why do you think Lily stayed in the marriage? Her father would drag her back. Even though he never liked Jerry, no one murders his son-in-law."

Raina thought about Lily and Cat meeting in the

storage room. Was the affair Lily's chance for happiness in this depressing house? For all Raina knew, they could be discussing the wine. "What's the name of the wine with the hint of strawberries in the foyer? I liked it."

Sonny gave her a puzzled look. "Strawberries are forbidden in this house. Jerry is deathly allergic to them."

Raina gasped, her eyes widening in shock. What if the killer added strawberry juice to the wine? It was certainly easier to transport than poison. "Does your brother have an EpiPen?"

"Yes, he carried it with him everywhere."

"You searched his pockets. Did you find one on him?"

Sonny stiffened in understanding. His expression gave nothing away, but the eyes darkened with murderous intent.

Raina shivered. What would he do if he found the killer before the police did?

"Excuse me, miss. The detective wishes to speak with you," the police officer called out from the doorway. "He's in the dining room."

As Raina dragged herself toward the doorway, her mind whirled. Where was Jerry's EpiPen? Did the killer take it? And how much should she tell the detective?

7

THE BROKEN WINE GLASS

As Raina headed toward the dining room, the commotion at the entryway caught her attention. She spun around and peered at all the comings and goings. Uniformed officials were everywhere and moving freely around the mansion. This couldn't be good for Nine Dragons business.

She stuck her head inside the ballroom. The servants and musicians were cleaning up. The untouched birthday cake stood in the corner of the buffet table like a forgotten wallflower. The guests were probably on their way home or asleep in one of the mansion's many guest rooms. The head housekeeper seemed to run this house with the efficiency of a drill sergeant.

The detective stood when she came in the dining room. He was close to six feet, a little on the heavier side with gray-blue eyes and iron-gray hair. He was probably her mother's age and liked to spend time outdoors—without sunblock. His dark tan camouflaged his age spots, but there was no hiding the network of deep crow's feet around his eyes. If she squinted, he looked like a cousin of Paul Newman. She could see her grandma fanning herself around this man.

He gestured for Raina to take a seat next to him rather than across the dining room table. So he wanted to pretend they were having a cozy chat—at two in the morning. "I am Detective David Bibb. And you are"—he glanced at the notebook in front of him—"Raina Sun, Sonny Kwan's fiancée?" At her nod, he continued, "Is this your first visit to the Kwan family home?"

"Yes."

"How long have you known the family?"

"I've only known Sonny since the beginning of the year," Raina said.

Detective Bibb nodded. He probably already knew the answers to most of his questions. "Tell me what happened tonight."

Raina hesitated. Which version of the evening should she tell him? If he found out she lied later on, would it be considered perjury? "We were in the middle of dinner when a servant came in and made a shocking comment." She described the dinner scene, the impromptu meeting in the library with the male members of the Kwan family, and what happened downstairs in the kitchen.

"Are you saying Lily Kwan and Cat Hernandez are having an affair?"

"I don't know."

"But what is your impression?"

"There's a connection, but I don't make judgments this early in an investigation."

Detective Bibb raised an eyebrow, his pen pausing

over his notepad. "Your grandma told me you're a private investigator in training."

Raina grimaced inwardly. Great. Next he would tell her to butt out of his case.

"I could use your help. You have an 'in' with the Kwan family," Detective Bibb said, nodding to himself. "This would be strictly confidential. You can't tell your grandma though. She doesn't look like the type who can keep a secret."

Raina perked up. "Seriously? You want my help?"

Detective Bibb's hand slapped the table. "No! I don't need another witness telling me how to do my job."

Raina jumped at the noise. He fooled her for a second. What happened in the interview with her grandma? "You're the professional here." Her voice came out squeaker than normal. "What else do you want to know?"

He scowled as if he was waiting for an argument. "I can detain you for withholding information from the police." His tone was brisk. No more Mr. Nice Cop. "There's more to this story than what you told me."

Raina hadn't planned on withholding information, but she no longer trusted him. What if he mentioned her name to the wrong person in the triad? It could start a chain reaction ending with her at the bottom of a lake. Unfortunately, Sonny was right. Her position as his fiancée was too precarious. And even if she were to take the risk, she would never gamble with her grandma's safety.

"Why don't we start at the beginning?" Detective Bibb said. "What did you do on your arrival?"

Raina told him about the exchange where Jerry Kwan

called her a high-class hooker, the meet and greet, Sonny's reaction to the clock, and how Cat caught Raina and Sonny making out. All of which were technically true.

"So you went upstairs to change your shoes, and Sonny went to get rid of the clock? Then he joined you upstairs?"

She nodded.

"Really, Miss Sun? A clock?"

"Yes, a clock. Kwan Gong would fall over with a heart attack."

Detective Bibb still had a doubtful look on his face.

"It's a Chinese thing. It's super bad luck for an elderly person to get a clock or watch as a birthday gift. It signifies his time is running out."

"Who would give such a taboo gift?"

"I don't know the family well enough to even guess. My interaction with the Kwans is through Sonny."

"Do you think Sonny killed his brother?" the detective asked.

"Now, Detective, that's an unfair question."

"What do you know about the Nine Dragons politics?"

"Not much. It's like every family business..." Raina's voice trailed off at the look the detective gave her. "Okay, maybe not like your average family business, but close enough. The older generation wants to keep things as is while the younger generation wants to modernize."

The detective spent the next few minutes trying to trip her up with creative roundabout questions.

Raina sagged back against the chair. She repeated her

statement, sticking to the truth but skirting the incident at the alcove.

Detective Bibb closed his notebook. He leaned back in his chair, tapping his pen on the table. "One more question, Miss Sun, and then you can leave."

Raina straightened. Finally!

He paused, glancing down at his notebook one more time. "Why is your wineglass next to Jerry Kwan's body?"

She swallowed, coughing at her dry mouth. "What wine glass?" she choked out.

"Good night, Miss Sun. Hopefully, the next time we meet, I'll have the warrant for your arrest."

RAINA SWEPT out of the dining room with her head held high. Once she was in the hallway and out of sight, her legs wobbled. She would have fallen if she didn't hold onto the wall for support.

The detective couldn't be serious. What motive did she have for killing Jerry? Or did he want to push her buttons to see if she would crack? She took a deep breath and pushed off from the wall, forcing herself into a nonchalant stroll. She could fall apart in private.

As she passed the library, Sonny stepped out and headed toward the dining room. They met halfway. The police officer was still at his post by the door, keeping an eye on the family.

"Everything okay?" Sonny whispered.

Raina nodded. "Any idea where I can find my grandma?"

"She's probably sleeping in your suite."

"We need to talk tomorrow. Good night." She nodded at him, but he gave her a quick hug.

"Thanks for everything," he whispered in her ear.

Raina stiffened. Geez, did they have to put on the lovebird show every time they were in public? She glanced over Sonny's shoulder. The officer watched them from the doorway.

They parted ways, and Raina headed upstairs. When she passed the intersection connecting the two wings of the house, she averted her gaze to avoid the alcove where Jerry had died a few hours ago. The low hum of conversation sounded as if half a dozen officials were still processing the crime scene.

Raina picked up her pace and trotted into her assigned suite. She flipped the lock and dropped her useless shoes on the floor. A soft snore from the bed caught her attention. Her grandma had wrapped the sheet around herself like a hot dog. Sleep sounded like heaven at the moment. There would be time enough to think later.

When Raina got up later that morning, it was close to noon. Po Po was nowhere in sight. She did her morning business and used the phone on the nightstand to call her grandma's cell phone.

"Hey, where are you?" Raina asked.

"Eating on the patio. The lunch buffet is better than anything you can find in Las Vegas. A few of the overnight guests are still here. You better come down quick if you want to talk to them," Po Po said.

Raina hung up and got dressed in a blouse and Capris. She transferred everything from her evening purse to her regular purse—a cross body hobo bag big enough to carry weapons of mass destruction. Her outfit had these faux pockets only big enough to carry a toothpick.

At the intersection connecting the two wings, she paused, glancing around. No one in sight; everyone must be at lunch. Before she could lose her nerve, she trotted toward the alcove. Her heart rate increased with each step.

The sunlight filtered in through the large picture windows on either side of the stone bench, highlighting patches of the carpet. It was quiet like someone put an upside-down fishbowl over this part of the house. No hum of an air conditioner or the faint sound of someone moving about. There was no hint a death had occurred at this spot a few hours ago. The servants had cleaned the residues of the crime while she'd slept.

Raina wished she had joss sticks to light for Jerry's spirit. She could probably find some in the mansion, but it was Lily's job as the wife to the eldest son to take care of the ancestors and her deceased husband.

She bowed her head and said a heartfelt prayer. She didn't know Jerry beyond their brief interactions the evening before, but he didn't deserve to die the way he did. Using someone's food allergy against him wasn't honorable—though there was no honor in murder to begin with.

She glanced around. Several closed doors lined the hall behind her, but not the segment in front where Jerry had appeared. She walked along the wall, looking for a panel that would open to a servant passageway like the one to the kitchen. He had stumbled onto her too suddenly for there not to be one. Her hands pushed on the wall, hoping to release a spring mechanism or a hidden doorknob. Approximately fifteen feet from the stone bench she hit the jackpot.

A panel sprung open, and a staircase led downstairs. But unlike the other servant staircase, this one was narrow and dark with no light bulb for illumination. A servant wouldn't be able to lug a tea set or a load of laundry up and down these stairs. Nope, this wasn't a typical servant stairway.

She stepped inside and inspected the doorframe behind her. A candlestick stuck out from the wall. When she wiggled the metal holder, something clicked, and the panel started to swing shut. She stopped the panel from closing. A release mechanism from the inside. A secret passage just like her grandma had predicted.

Raina popped her head back into the hall. Still empty. Time for a little exploring. She stepped back and shut the panel. If her hand wasn't holding the candlestick holder, she might have panicked at the sudden darkness. She stood still to let her eyes adjust and dug out a hair stick from her purse. She pressed the hidden button on the charm like her grandma had demonstrated and the flashlight lit a small area in front in her. She grinned. Just like Nancy Drew.

She inched down the staircase, sweeping the beam on the ground in front of her and on the wall. Cobwebs, dust, and more shadows. A single set of footprints—had to be Jerry's—headed toward the main hallway she had just left. She stepped around them, so as not to smear his prints. The prints weren't evenly placed, which meant he probably stumbled around in here, seeking escape or help. A dying man's last dance.

Raina shivered and focused on the investigation rather than the death. What was Jerry doing here? Who else knew about it, and where did it lead? The air was stale and heavy. A scratching noise whispered at her from the walls. Rats? She swept the beam of light around. No droppings. But there were plenty of spiderwebs, which meant there were plenty of spiders. The hair on the back of her neck stiffened. Her skin crawled as if spiders dropped from the ceiling.

Raina gritted her teeth and marched down the stairs. She was letting her imagination take the reins. The darkness and silence had better end soon. Her hands grew grimy from the handrail. Yuck!

The staircase ended in a landing area with walls on all sides like a small closet. Instead of a single set of footprints, there were more than one set. However, she couldn't tell if the other set of smeared prints belonged to a man or woman. Against the far wall, a broken wine glass glinted back at her from the floor. The wine dried into a dark pool around it. Bingo! The murder weapon.

8

SALTING A WOUND

Raina was surprised to find the murder weapon. It was sloppy for the killer to leave this critical evidence behind, but maybe he or she thought no one would find it. After all, the secret passage was secret for a reason. While it wasn't unusual for a guest to walk around with a broken wineglass, it would be memorable.

She swept the beam of light on the surrounding walls, looking for a lever to open the panel to the main part of the house. Nothing. Maybe there was a button, but she couldn't see it from this distance with her feeble light. If she stepped on the landing, she would smear the footprints even more and contaminate the real crime scene. And her cell phone was broken so she couldn't even take a picture. How the heck did detectives investigate a murder without a smartphone back in the day?

As Raina made her way back upstairs and toward the patio, her mind raced. If she told Sonny about this secret passageway, would he insist on checking it out and possibly contaminating the crime scene accidentally...or intentionally? Even if Sonny had nothing to do with his brother's death, he still wouldn't want to invite the police back into his home. She was almost sure he would want to solve his brother's murder, but his means of achieving this and what he might do with the information could be...questionable.

If she called the police, she would end up on Sonny's bad side. And the last thing she wanted was to come this close to her grandfather's journal only to lose it again. This might be her last chance to shine a light at the skeleton in her family's closet. An image of Po Po's face flashed in front of her. Forget about the rest of the family, Raina would risk anything for her beloved grandma's peace of mind.

A servant stood at the bottom of the staircase, clearing the birthday gifts from the side table in the foyer. He directed Raina to the French doors that led to the patio where the lunch buffet was held. Even before she crossed the threshold, conversation and clinking silverware drifted toward her.

Raina surveyed the scene. The patio was a square, protruding from the house like a peninsula. On the right was a buffet table with one server standing behind it. A few remaining houseguests sat at the five large round tables with teal umbrellas.

Po Po and Kwan Gong chatted with two other couples their age at the table closest to the buffet. Her grandma pulled cans of Red Bull from her purse and distributed them around the table. Oh great. The senior citizens would bounce off the walls within an hour.

Raina grabbed a plate of food and headed toward

Freddie and Myling Low at the table furthest from everyone else. The Lows didn't look like they wanted company, but this technicality didn't bother Raina. She would be hard-pressed to find an excuse to interview them once they left the mansion.

Freddie scowled like he chewed on gravel instead of the smoked salmon and rice pilaf on his plate. He had changed out of his black tux and wore a buttoned shirt, cargo shorts, and sandals. With the glare of the morning sun highlighting every wrinkle and gray hair, he looked every bit his age—mid-forties and going downhill fast. He glanced at his wife with concern and whispered something to her.

Myling shook her head. She had a slight grayish tint to her face like she had been sick. She pushed her plate a foot away from her and clutched the cloth napkin on her lap, twisting it around her fingers. She was as lovely as last night, and even more so with the husband as a contrast. She'd changed out of her party dress, opting for a long white Maxi dress and rhinestone sandals. Did she drive around with a change of clothes in the trunk of her car? The couple looked like a walking advertisement for a beach resort. Or a Viagra commercial.

Raina clunked her plate on the table, flashing the couple a bright smile. "Mind if I join you?" She sat down without waiting for an answer. Her stomach gurgled, but she ignored it. "Are you okay, Myling?"

Freddie threw his napkin on the table. He ignored Raina and addressed his wife. "I shouldn't have let you talk me into coming to this party. Now the police will watch us because of Jerry's death, and we still don't have a solution for the Italian mob problem."

"Honey, this is not the time or place for this conversation." Myling patted her husband's arm. "Can you ask a servant to get me a cup of warm lemon water?"

"I'll go get it myself," Freddie said grudgingly. He kissed Myling's hand and headed toward the house, passing Cat on her way toward the lunch buffet.

Raina shoved a forkful of smoked salmon into her mouth so her stomach would stop complaining. Mmmm... She eyed the shrimp skewers. Too much work to slide the shrimp off the stick. She dug into the rice pilaf instead. Her stomach did a little happy dance.

"There's no need to rub it in," Myling said.

Raina glanced at the other woman. "Excuse me?" she asked, barely getting the words out around the food in her mouth.

"You're just having too good of a time with the food over there," Myling said. She still eyed the food on her plate like it was rancid.

"I'm sorry?" Raina said. Did Myling have a stomach bug?

"How did you meet Sonny?" Myling asked, changing the subject. "A girl like you doesn't seem to be the type to hang out with triad leaders."

Raina finished chewing. Like that, huh? So Sonny's plan to make his ex jealous worked. "We clicked when we met in San Francisco earlier this year."

"You guys have been together that long? Jerry said the engagement was a farce."

Since Myling was in a sharing mood, Raina asked, "So how did you meet your husband? Was it love at first sight?" What she wanted to ask was why a beautiful young woman would marry a middle-aged triad leader? She could have had the same kind of life with Sonny.

Myling raised an eyebrow. "Wouldn't you rather ask why I left Sonny?"

"What makes you think I don't know?"

"I doubt it. Sonny keeps everything close to his chest."

Raina wasn't sure about this assessment. Sonny had been chatty enough with her. "Okay, I'll bite. Why did you leave him? I'm sure your husband is a nice guy, but Sonny is...uh...." Younger and hotter?

"Closer to my age?"

Raina nodded.

"Sonny wasn't in love with me. He wanted the marriage because my family owns half the cloud storage companies in Asia." Myling gave Raina a pointed look. "Your family owns Wong International Shipping. You should know how it is."

"Things are different between Sonny and me."

"If you say so." Myling's expression said otherwise.

A shadow fell across the table. Raina glanced up to find Sonny standing next to her holding a plate of food. He pulled out a chair and sat.

"What are you two ladies chattering about?" Sonny asked, unfolding the cloth napkin.

"You," Myling winked at him. "Are your ears burning yet?" Her face had lost the grayish tint while she talked to Raina, and now it positively glowed as she eyed Sonny.

He was dressed in a manner similar to Freddie. Polo shirt and Bermuda shorts. A Rolex adorned his right hand. A lefty. While the sunlight highlighted the silvery scar on his face, it also added a warmth and youthfulness missing from Freddie's. Did Myling regret her choice?

Sonny slung an arm around the back of Raina's chair and leaned across her. "Save the teasing for Freddie. Only Raina gets to tease me now." He gave Raina a broad smile and lowered his voice. "Morning, sleepyhead. How come you sneaked off before I got out of the shower?"

Raina reached for her glass of water, hoping it would hide her snicker. Seriously? He wanted to pretend they spent the night together for his ex? Were they still in high school? She kissed him on the cheek. This would cost him extra.

"We had to come downstairs to see the guests off," she said. "But we can always shower together later."

Sonny chuckled appreciatively. He picked up his fork and tipped his chin. "Freddie better keep his day job. He would make a horrible waiter."

Raina sipped on her water, glancing over Myling's shoulder

Freddie approached the table, holding a steaming mug with both hands. He stiffened when he laid eyes on Sonny, but set the mug gingerly in front of his wife. For someone who had the power to cash in a favor from the Dai Lo of the Nine Dragons triad, Freddie didn't look like he had the upper hand. Did Jerry's death throw him off balance? Or was it finding his young wife chatting with her ex?

"It's not every day we get to have lunch with a murder suspect," Freddie said, sitting next to his wife.

Raina choked mid-sip and tears filled her eyes. Freddie certainly went straight for the jugular.

Sonny rubbed her back until she stopped coughing. "Are you okay, Rainy?" At her nod, he addressed Freddie. "Being a murderer suspect is not a novelty for either of us. There's no need to scare the women." His tone was flat even though he smiled with dazzling brilliance.

"Afraid to lose another one at the altar?" Freddie asked.

Raina sighed inwardly and kept eating. This wasn't the time to bring the subject of the secret passage to Sonny.

Myling's eyes danced with amusement. Apparently, she enjoyed verbal sparring between the men. She rolled her eyes and addressed Raina. "Boys will be boys."

Raina swallowed her bite. Did those words really come out of Myling's mouth? If they were having a cozy chat, they might as well make it worthwhile. "Did you see Jerry last night before dinner? Did you notice anything unusual about him?"

"We chatted with Jerry in the foyer like everyone else," Freddie said. "The two of you spent more time with him than we did."

"Were the two of you in the ballroom the entire time before dinner?" Raina asked. "Did you notice anyone leaving?"

Myling's face softened into a satisfied smile, and her husband placed a protective hand on her flat stomach. "I had to use the restroom. Morning sickness can strike at any time during the day."

Raina's heart sank. Yikes! She glanced at Sonny, but she couldn't read his expression.

Myling placed a hand on the side of her mouth, mock whispering to Raina. "Don't let Sonny talk you into starting a family too soon. Enjoy your time as a newlywed first." She stood. "We should give our condolences to

Kwan Gong." She linked hands with her husband, and the couple strolled away.

Sonny's jaw tightened, and he signaled for the server to avoid looking at the beaming couple chatting with his grandfather.

"Are you okay?" Raina asked.

Sonny glanced at her. "Why wouldn't I be?"

"I'm just making sure."

"Don't worry about me. Freddie's dirty hands will come back to haunt him eventually."

Raina hadn't meant Freddie's business dealings. If Sonny wanted to ignore the pregnancy, she wasn't forcing him to discuss it. "Is the Nine Dragons helping Freddie with the Italian mob?"

"We didn't get around to discussing business last night. Did you find anything on the murder?"

Raina bit her lower lip. This was it. The moment of truth. She should tell him about the secret passage. "What did you do with the clock last night?" Okay, she was stalling.

"I hid it in a storage room."

"Did you see anyone while you were down there?" Raina asked, thinking of Cat and Lily. Maybe he already knew about their affair. She would hate to be the one to bring this to light. "It would help if you have an alibi."

Sonny threw his cloth napkin on the table. "I already told you I have nothing to do with my brother's death." He stalked back into the house without another word.

Raina's eyes widened. Whoa! Talk about pushing the wrong buttons. Was he upset about Jerry's death or Myling's pregnancy? Whatever the issue was, she didn't sign up to be an armchair therapist for Sonny.

At least this solved her dilemma about the secret passage. Not her fault he didn't stay to hear her out. She caught her grandma's eye and gestured for them to return to the house. It was time to call the police and tell them about the murder weapon.

9

THE DRAGON'S LAIR

Instead of heading upstairs with her grandma, Raina got roped into helping Kwan Gong see the remaining guests off. She did her duty as Sonny's fiancée and accepted condolences like they meant something to her. Once the last car headed away from the house on the driveway, Kwan Gong said Raina and her grandma could make themselves at home and locked himself in the library.

Po Po turned to Raina. "Why do you have cobwebs in your hair?"

Raina brushed her ponytail with her hands. "You couldn't have told me this earlier?"

"I didn't want to draw attention to it."

"Yes, I can see why saying nothing would be better." Raina didn't bother hiding the sarcasm in her voice.

"I thought it would establish you as an eccentric in the Kwan family. You can get away with murder if you're eccentric."

Raina gave her grandma a sideways glance. She didn't

even know how to respond to the comment, so she ignored it. "I found a secret passage just like you suspected." She told her grandma about the broken wineglass she'd found and her conversation with Sonny and Myling. "I should call Detective Bibb."

"Sonny wouldn't want the police snooping around the family home again." The smile slipped off her grandma's face. "I don't want him angry at you."

"I can always play the bimbo card when he finds out."

"Now that would be a great excuse. I'm too stupid to live. Kill me now." Po Po fluttered her lashes like a twitching bug on steroids.

Raina burst out laughing. "Okay, maybe it won't work, but I have to do what is right. Let's go upstairs and pack up. We can use your cell phone in private there."

They didn't encounter anyone on their way upstairs, and their footsteps echoed in the hallway. Raina inched a little closer to her grandma. The house was already in mourning.

At the intersection leading to the east wing of the house, Raina glanced at the alcove where Jerry had died. A white wreath of roses lay on the bench. Where were the joss sticks? What if his spirit hung around the place waiting for his family to honor his death? She shivered and turned away.

Inside the guest bedroom suite, Raina dialed the number for the detective, turning her back to her grandma and looking out the window at the rolling green lawn outside. Back in California, the lawn would have been a brownish gold with the watering restrictions from the drought.

Two Dobermans led a guard along the fence line at a

distance. Although she couldn't see any firearms, he was probably heavily armed. She turned away from the view. Either the Kwan family was a paranoid bunch, or they needed this level of security from their enemies. She bet they dealt with the latter like movie stars did with the paparazzi.

Someone picked up the phone. "Detective David Bibb."

Raina hesitated. Making this call would signal to the police she wasn't in the Nine Dragon's pocket. Would the detective use this against her in the future?

"Hello?" Detective Bibb said. "Is this a prank call? Do I need to trace the line?"

Raina cleared her throat. "Hi, this is Raina Sun." She spilled the beans about the secret passage at the Kwan mansion. When she was done, there was silence at the other end of the line. It stretched out for two heartbeats before he finally spoke.

"Does Sonny Kwan know about this call?" Detective Bibb asked.

"No. Please don't mention my name."

"I see." He was silent again, letting it stretch out for another minute. "Thank you, Miss Sun. I know you put yourself at great risk by calling me, and I appreciate it."

Raina hung up, feeling a load lift from her shoulders she hadn't known was there. Being on the wrong side of the law, even if only for appearances, bothered her. She wasn't a Miss Goody Two Shoes, but she believed in the justice system.

She turned to see her grandma standing next to Sonny and Cat. She didn't know which was worse—Cat's mocking smirk or the tightness around Sonny's eyes. He tried too hard to have an unreadable expression, but it only magnified his suppressed anger. Her mouth went dry. She swallowed and attempted to smile.

Sonny kept his eyes on Raina but addressed Po Po. "My grandfather wants to speak with you before you leave. He's in the library. Cat, go with her so she doesn't get lost."

"Tell him I'll be down in a minute," Po Po said, clearly trying to stall so Raina wouldn't be alone with Sonny.

He turned to look at her grandma. "Go, now. I need to talk to Rainy alone."

Po Po tipped her chin up at him. "You're not throwing my granddaughter into a lake without me."

He blinked. "So are you proposing to help me?" His voice lost its earlier edge. "I'll hold her arms, and you can grab her legs? No thanks. Cat can help me with the grunt work."

Her grandma got into a fighting stance, clutching the pimp cane in front of her "Are you mocking me, young man?" She gave the cane a whirl.

Cat jumped back with a start. "Hey, watch it!"

Sonny sighed. "Just go before I change my mind about the lake."

Raina gave her grandma an encouraging smile. "I'll be fine." The knot in her stomach grew tighter.

Po Po and Cat headed toward the door.

"Why don't you let me hold your cane?" Cat said, holding out her hand.

"You'll have to pry it from my cold dead hands," her grandma replied.

"I can arrange..."

They walked further away from the bedroom, and Raina couldn't hear the rest of Cat's reply.

Sonny shook his head sadly. "I wish you trusted me enough to come to me first."

"Ah, trust you about what?" Raina asked.

His lips curled with disgust. "Drop the act. I hate dumb girls, and you're not a good actress."

Raina's stomach heaved, and she had to force her voice to sound normal. "What do you expect? Given your reputation and your family? You weren't honorable in our past dealings. I have no proof you're not involved in your brother's death. For all I know, you're using me to throw off the investigation."

"So my word isn't good enough for you?"

"I don't trust anyone when it comes to murder."

Sonny studied her as if weighing her worth. "Follow me. I've got proof of my innocence." He turned and left the room.

By the time Raina crossed the threshold, Sonny's longer legs had carried him halfway down the hall. She ran to catch up with him. He didn't say anything while they made their way downstairs past the kitchen and the storage rooms and out a side door.

He strode through the courtyard without glancing at the hanging linen or the discarded boxes from the grocery delivery. A servant straightened, dropping his cigarette on the ground, and nodded at them.

Sonny continued through the small brick archway that led to a small cottage hidden from view on the driveway. There weren't any video cameras around the cottage. He probably didn't need any because the cottage was so close to the main house.

Besides, it would be disturbing to record the family as they went about their business at home. Anyone who could make it through the wrought iron fence, Dobermans, and armed patrols had to be family or friend. There was no security in the world good enough to protect you from the enemy within.

Sonny punched in several numbers on the keypad on top of the doorknob, and a lock clicked open. He threw open the door, gesturing for her to step inside. With the sun behind the building, the interior was in shadows.

Raina glanced behind her. The servant had gone back inside the main house. Her grandma wouldn't know to look here for her. She glanced at Sonny who watched her with a bemused smirk, almost as if daring her to proceed.

She took a deep breath to steady her nerves. It would take more than a bad temper to keep her from seeing what proof he had. She stepped inside. Before her eyes could adjust to the dim interior, Sonny closed the door and slid the lock home with a loud bang.

RAINA TIGHTENED the grip on her purse. It took all her willpower to stand still until her eyes adjusted, and she could see the outlines of the furniture in the room.

Sonny clicked on a light and crossed the room to a leather armchair next to the stone fireplace. He grabbed a remote from the side table and pushed a button. A screen dropped from the opposite wall. "Welcome to my dragon's lair. This is my hideout and where I run the family business." He pulled a wireless keyboard onto his lap and tapped on it.

Raina perched on the edge of the smaller armchair across from Sonny. It was much too small for a man, but maybe that was the intent—whoever sat across from Sonny would be uncomfortable the entire time.

The room was a typical man-cave with leather and dark wood tones. Not much different from the decor of the library in the main house, except these books along the wall looked well read. What if her grandfather's journal was hidden in this room? She squinted at the books on the shelves, looking for the distinct Chinese longevity symbol on the spine and front of the leather cover.

"You can stop squinting. I wouldn't put your grandfather's journal somewhere that anyone could just walk off with it," Sonny said.

Raina pressed her lips together. There was no point in denying his assessment. She glanced at the twelve video feeds on the screen. In the top corner, Raina and Sonny parted ways in the foyer last night.

"Look at the time stamp," he said.

She glanced at the time. For the next few minutes, she watched him come back up from the storage room and chat with a person in the ballroom. A servant came by and whispered in his ear. Sonny glanced at the watch on his wrist and strolled through the double doors of the ballroom.

"I left to look for you," Sonny said.

In the video, he headed up the stairs. Time passed and then Raina and Sonny made their way into the ballroom with Cat behind them.

Sonny stopped the videos. "There are no cameras upstairs, but the time stamp shows I was in the ballroom the entire time you were upstairs. You can also question anyone I spoke to."

Raina got up to stand next to the bookshelves, pretending she needed to stretch her legs. Her gaze scanned the shelves again before she turned around to address him. "You're a crime boss. You don't need to get your hands dirty. That's what lackeys are for. I'm sure Cat would shoot on command."

"You think it's that easy to hire a hitman to take out my brother in our family home?" His tone sounded incredulous. "You give me far too much credit, Rainy."

"You didn't answer my question about Cat."

"I didn't tell her to kill my brother."

"Could she have killed Jerry on her own? Maybe she wants to help consolidate your power," Raina said.

"I highly doubt it. Cat is Jerry's man."

Raina tipped her head at the retracted screen. "Do the video feeds clear Cat from Jerry's death?" If her loyalty belonged to Jerry, then what was she doing with Lily down in the storage room?

"I haven't had time to check."

"Does anyone else monitor the video feed? The guard by the gate?"

Sonny shook his head. "It gets recorded, but no one looks at it unless we have a party where we invite questionable people."

"Like the Lows at your grandfather's party?"

He squinted at one of the screens. "The police are at the gate. I need you to stall them until I can join you."

"What are you going to do?"

"Call my lawyer."

Raina's jaw dropped. "You have a lawyer?"

"On speed dial." Sonny's tone was dry, and he pulled out his cell phone. "You can't be a master criminal without one these days."

As she headed toward the door, Raina's gaze drifted to a tan leather spine on the last bookshelf. She pretended to stumble and fell down to her knees.

The armchair creaked behind her. "Are you okay?" Sonny called out.

Raina picked herself up, chuckling to hide her excitement. She had seen enough. Hopefully, he would think she was embarrassed. "I'm such a klutz."

Once outside, Raina paused but couldn't hear Sonny's conversation with his lawyer. She rubbed her sore knee, but the fall had been worth it. She got close enough to see the Chinese longevity symbol on the spine of the leather book. The same symbol on her grandfather's journal.

10

A PASSION

As Raina trudged toward the main house, she thought about her conversation with Sonny. Were the cameras for recording the comings and goings of the senior members in the Nine Dragons? She glanced at all the windows glinting in the sunlight. The mansion had presence and beauty, but it was empty where it counted.

The narrow downstairs hallway thrummed with activity. Clinking and clanking from different parts of this workspace. Chinese music played from a radio. Wait! Was that Po Po's voice?

Raina stuck her head into the kitchen. Po Po directed the kitchen staff to set up tea in one of the many sitting rooms. Her grandma acknowledged her but finished her conversation before joining Raina.

"The police are driving up from the gate," Raina said. As they headed upstairs, she filled her grandma in on the conversation with Sonny.

"The journal was right there? How come you didn't snatch it?" Po Po asked.

"Because I don't want him to manhandle me. I can't outmuscle him."

"So how do you plan to outwit him?"

"I don't. I plan to do a little B&E at the next opportunity," Raina said, holding open the panel for her grandma.

Po Po stepped into the hallway on the main floor. "How are we going to break into his office when we are leaving tonight? You're not really his fiancée."

"You're my secret weapon. I'm hoping you can turn your charm on Kwan Gong. I'm counting on you to get us another invitation to the mansion."

Po Po saluted smartly, tapping her heels together. "Oh, yeah. He's not going to even know what hit him. I wonder where I can find a supply of the little blue pill around here."

Raina covered her ears. "La-la-la."

"I might as well get a little fun out of this."

"He doesn't look to be in good shape. Just don't put him in the hospital with your hip gyrations."

Her grandma snickered, pleased with Raina's assessment of her prowess in the bedroom.

Raina suppressed a smirk. It didn't take much to make her grandma happy.

They passed the ballroom and crossed the foyer in time to see a servant leading Detective Bibb into the mansion. Raina and her grandma shook hands with the detective, and they stood awkwardly until the servant led them into a sitting room to the right of the main door.

Once everyone had a seat, Detective Bibb asked, "Will anyone from the family join us?"

"Sonny will once he gets off the phone with his lawyer," Raina said.

"Oh, great," Detective Bibb mumbled to himself. He glanced at Raina. "What can you tell me?"

"Not much more than what I already told you on the phone. I found out Jerry had a strawberry allergy, and I tasted strawberries in the wine."

Detective Bibb jotted the information in his notebook. "Did anyone else have this wine?"

"I don't know," Raina said. "Is there anything you could share with us?"

"Ms. Sun, this could potentially be a homicide investigation. You're not a professional"—he cut his eyes to Po Po who opened her mouth to protest—"even though you have a few encounters with murder, you are still a private citizen. I can't share information with you even if I want to. I'm not putting my job on the line to satisfy some amateur's curiosity."

"Who are you calling an amateur?" Po Po's sharp tone chilled the initial cordial atmosphere.

The rattle of a metal cart approached the sitting room. Cat came into the room pushing a tea cart laden with cakes and finger sandwiches. She had traded the tight black leather from last night for a white sundress. With her wavy brown hair and natural brown tan, she could have been a PTA mom in an alternate dimension.

Raina did a double take. She hadn't expected a murder suspect to show up with goodies. Cat's loose yellow cardigan undoubtedly hid the shoulder holster for her gun.

The henchwoman handed out tea and cakes like she had been doing this her entire life. She had assumed one of those blank expressions often found on servants who tried to blend into the background. Geez, did she think they were stupid and wouldn't notice her eavesdropping?

The detective scowled at them. "Do I have a sign on my forehead that says 'go ahead and waste my day?' Now where is this secret passage?"

Footsteps approached the sitting room. Sonny came into view. "Good afternoon. My lawyer is on his way, so unless you have a search warrant, Detective Bibb, you might as well have some cake and tea during the wait."

Detective Bibb scowled at Sonny. "How long?"

"Twenty minutes, more or less," Sonny said, accepting a cup of tea from Cat.

"Are you kidding me? In twenty minutes someone could contaminate the crime scene. Someone could be cleaning up while we're here eating cake."

"I guess that's a risk we'll have to take," Sonny said. His tone held a twinge of mild regret.

Detective Bibb stood. "Even though it's Sunday, I can find a judge to get me a search warrant under the circumstances. And when I have it in my hand, I will be searching more than just this secret passage."

The two men stared at each other to the exclusion of everyone else in the room, playing a mental game of chicken. Po Po watched the two men with a gleeful expression on her face. She was probably mentally egging them on like a child on a schoolyard fight.

Raina set her teacup on the coffee table. "Sonny, hon, this isn't the time for the police to crawl all over the house." She glanced at the detective. "We're in mourning. Please try to be sensitive to our situation."

Sonny nodded reluctantly. Not that he had a choice. Raina felt a twinge of guilt for calling the detective.

As they headed upstairs, Sonny reached out and held her hand. Was this a gesture of his anxiety or playacting on his part?

When she got to the section of upstairs hallway that led to the secret passage, she hesitated. She didn't want to tip her hand by using the light on the hair sticks. "I forgot to mention that we would need flashlights."

Sonny and Cat reached into their pockets and pulled out pencil flashlights. The detective pulled one out of his pocket as well. It seemed everyone read their Boy Scout manual.

Raina opened the panel on the wall. "The wineglass is at the end of this staircase."

As Sonny's beam of light swept in front of them, anxiety settled in Raina's stomach. She was worried about their reaction when they saw the wine glass. What if they didn't come to the same conclusion she did? Would they think she had an overactive imagination?

The others shuffled behind them, loud enough to scare away any remaining evil spirit. Raina's chest tightened. Something was wrong, but she couldn't pinpoint what bothered her. With so many flashlights, the staircase was less intimidating than before. Her hand gripped the grimy rail as they inched down the stairs.

It wasn't until the beam from Sonny's flashlight landed on the floor that she figured out what was bothering her. The dust didn't swirl and whirl like it did before. Either her memory was going to pot or someone had come here after she did. They reached the end of the passage. Several beams of light swept across the clean floor.

"Where is the wine glass?" Po Po asked.

Where indeed. Raina gave Sonny a sideways glance. He appeared confused and relieved at the same time. If he wasn't the one to clean up the mess, then who did?

WITHOUT A SEARCH WARRANT, Detective Bibb left, mumbling about a wild goose chase. The servants brought down their overnight bags, and a chauffeur pulled the cherry-red convertible Po Po had rented into the circular driveway. Evidently, Raina and her grandma had overstayed their welcome.

During the drive back to Toronto, Raina gripped the steering wheel until her white knuckles stood out against the black leather. Appearing like a fool in front of the detective didn't bother her as much as her misplaced trust in Sonny. She'd thought they were on the same team, but they had been playing on two different fields the entire time.

"Are you done mumbling to yourself?" Po Po asked.

"I should have guarded the secret passage instead of following Sonny to his lair. How did he have enough time to clean up the crime scene when he was with me in the office?" Raina asked.

"Cat."

"Wasn't she with you in the library?"

"Nope. She disappeared after showing me into the room."

Raina smacked her palm against the steering wheel. So it was Cat! "If she cleaned up the crime scene, is she an accomplice or the murderer?"

"Maybe both. Or maybe neither. She could have cleaned up the crime scene because she thought she was helping Sonny."

"This doesn't compute for me. Sonny said Cat is Jerry's woman."

Po Po snorted. "Then why is she boinking her boss's wife?"

"We don't know this for sure. There might be nothing scandalous in their relationship."

"You can give them the benefit of a doubt, but I'm sticking to my opinion until proven otherwise. Did you talk to Lily? Maybe she wanted her husband dead so she could run off into the sunset with Cat."

Raina shook her head. "Lily is hiding in her room, but she is on my list of suspects though."

"Who else is on your list?"

"The Lows?"

"Freddie wants Sonny's help with the Italian mob problem, right? Why would he or Myling kill Jerry?"

"Who knows? Maybe they killed Jerry under the misguided notion that if they got rid of Sonny's internal problem, he would help them in return. Just because the Nine Dragons owes them a favor, doesn't mean Sonny would help them."

"Anyone else?" Po Po didn't bother to hide the doubt in her voice.

Raina shook her head. "I'm annoyed with myself for letting Sonny move me around like a chess piece. I was supposed to be his fiancée for one weekend, but now I have to find his brother's killer too."

"Nooo. He only wanted you to talk to the women involved in Jerry's life."

Raina gave her grandma a sideways glance. "You know I can't ask questions without getting involved." A combination of curiosity and strong interest in the Kwan family guaranteed she would be all over this case.

"Well, at least we'll have some exciting days ahead of us. Anything is better than walking around the block like a decrepit old lady," Po Po said. "Guess what?"

Raina glanced at her grandma and then back on the road. She chuckled at the twinkle in her grandma's eyes. Exciting was relative. "Do you have an excuse for us to go back to the mansion?"

"I have something even better. Lily is prostrated with grief, and you know we can't expect a man to see to the details." Po Po paused dramatically. "I volunteered to plan Jerry's memorial service."

"That's quick thinking. Now we can come and go as we please at the mansion for the next few days."

"Hey, don't put words into my mouth. I'm just trying to help my buddy out."

"When did you and Kwan Gong become bosom buddies?"

"When he confessed he was secretly in love with me fifty years ago." This time there was a self-satisfied smirk on her grandma's face.

"Every time we meet one of your old friends we stumble on another secret admirer. Geez, I didn't realize you were such a heartbreaker."

"Broken hearts are better than dead bodies."

"It's not my fault that my superpower attracts dead bodies. I wonder if I was a coroner in my previous life."

"Or a hangman."

Raina gave her grandma the stink eye. "Do we want to talk smack? Oh, master of disguise who can't decide between a washed up version of Madonna with the cone bra or a ninja."

"At least I have ambition." Po Po waved a hand in Raina's direction. "Girl, you need to find a passion."

"It's kind of hard to keep a man when a dead body appears every few months." Maybe the statement wasn't technically true, considering that Matthew was a homicide detective. He wouldn't propose if it were.

"You don't need a man. That's what batteries are for. I'm talking about what you want to do when you grow up."

"Oh, like a job? I'll figure it out when I finish my graduate degree in the winter."

"Nooo," Po Po said, stretching out the word. "A job is something you do to either kill time or because you need to make a living. Neither of which applies in this case. A passion is something you do that brings you joy even if it doesn't pay you."

"Po Po, my savings will run out. It's not like I could survive on odd jobs the rest of my life."

By Raina's calculations, if she continued her frugal lifestyle, she had another two years before she needed to find a real job again. "I must return to the cubicle world sooner or later."

Her engineering license was up for renewal this fall, and she planned to renew it. Though she would receive her graduate degree in Asian history by December, the prospect of a future job in this field was bleak. The degree had been a ploy to escape from her family in San Francisco, so it did its job.

"The day you return to a normal job is the day I would have to drown my sorrow in a bottle of vodka or a box of chocolate donuts." Po Po sounded glum.

"You'll find something else to keep you occupied. Maybe one of the cousins would need you to save them."

"It wouldn't be as much fun as chasing down leads with you. You should apply for the intern position with Moody Investigations. The ad in the *Gold Springs Weekly* said they are taking applicants until the end of the week."

Raina had seen the ad in their hometown's newspaper before they left for their trip to Toronto. "I can't. What if Matthew finds out?"

"So? Are you going to let a man dictate what you want to do? It's not like the two of you are in a relationship."

Raina told her grandma his idea of opening a private investigation firm and his offer to take her on as a non-paid secretary and apprentice. She left out his marriage proposal.

"I still don't see what the problem is," Po Po said.

"I can't reject him and turn around to work for a rival firm."

"You didn't reject him. You rejected his sucker's deal for a paid one."

"Let me think about it."

"If they call, say yes to the interview."

Raina's eyes widened. "You submitted an application for me?"

"Well, yeah. By the time you're done thinking about it,

they would have hired somebody else. So just say thanks and move on."

Raina harrumphed. Her grandmother was probably right. "Thanks." She tried to inject enthusiasm into her tone, but it fell flat. If she didn't submit an application, then they couldn't reject her. While she had some success as an amateur sleuth, she was nowhere ready for prime time. But with training, she could be ready or at least knowledgeable enough to hold her ground with Matthew.

11

A WHITE KNIGHT

Monday morning Raina and Po Po went their separate ways. Technically her grandma stayed at the apartment to make phone calls for the memorial service. If the Kwan family was to hold the service within three days of the death as tradition dictated, there was plenty of work for her grandma to do. Although, it was probably unrealistic for Jerry's body to be released in time to meet the deadline.

Raina spent the morning in the office of the Chinese Opera Company doing paperwork. When her grandma had proposed working for her friend this summer, Raina had assumed she would be a stagehand or an assistant on the set.

Instead, she spent most of her time in a one-room office next to the Chinese Cultural Centre with the office manager. Between the two of them, they did everything from entering the time for payroll to updating the company's website. Not exciting, but with another dead body, it was the perfect mindless summer job. If nothing else, she could add marketing to her resume.

When Raina clocked out at one, she texted Po Po to see if she wanted to have a late lunch. Her grandma replied an affirmative, and Raina swung by the apartment with the rental car.

"What are you in the mood for?" Po Po asked.

"How about sandwiches?" Raina asked, pulling away from the curb.

"From the cafe next to the cell phone store? Is this why you drove instead of walked to work today?" Po Po's voice was exasperated. "Rainy, you're spending your entire inheritance replacing phones. It's your third one this year."

"It's not my fault dead cell phones and dead bodies go hand-in-hand. I'm just lucky it's not cars. I definitely can't afford to replace those."

After lunch, Raina and her grandma spent the next hour at the cell phone store, going through all the options. She settled on a pay-as-you-go phone, using an app to forward her voicemail messages from her USA phone number to this temporary phone.

She would pay for two cell phone services, but she didn't want to put her USA cell phone number on hold in case Moody Investigations called her for an interview. It was a temporary solution, but hopefully she would return to the States by the end of the month.

When she opened her purse to hand over the pieces of her cell phone for recycling, her thoughts drifted to Jerry's cell phone. Sonny hadn't mentioned it since the night of the murder. She assumed he still had it. How could she get her hands on Jerry's phone?

Raina wrapped up the cell phone purchase, and they went outside.

"I wonder who this 'Mis' person is that Jerry exchanged explicit text messages with." Raina wondered out loud.

"It's probably his mistress. Men like Jerry always have a mistress. You need to be prepared if you marry Sonny."

"There's nothing between Sonny and me other than mutual...benefits."

"Just don't turn it into friends with benefits. You can't handle casual."

Raina groaned. Why did every conversation with her grandmother circle back to her love life? "Not that kind of benefits. Back on topic, how can we find out who Jerry's mistress is? Three women came out of the ballroom—Lily, Myling, and Cat. Lily is out. Myling is expecting her first child with her new husband. They are still in the honeymoon phase. It's more believable for Sonny and Myling to have an affair than for Jerry and Myling to have one. I guess that leaves Jerry and Cat."

"We're having dinner with the Kwans. We can ask Sonny or Lily if they have a name later." Po Po paused for a moment. "How do we know the mistress is a woman?"

"That's a good question. For all we know, Jerry and Freddie could be lovers," Raina said for her grandma's sake. She didn't think there was any truth to the statement.

Po Po's eyes gleamed, and she rubbed her hands together. "Ah, yes. This is turning out to be like an episode on the *Jerry Springer Show*. I like it!"

"While we're at it, what if Kwan Gong and Cat are having an affair, too?"

"Are you mocking me?"

Raina burst out laughing. "I can't help it if you like the musical beds theory. Is this what you seniors do when the lights are off at the senior center?"

Po Po turned prim. "We're all consenting adults. And it's none of your business."

"Okay. I don't really want to know anyway. We better leave in an hour if we want time to chitchat before dinner. I want to hear what Lily has to say about her husband's death."

"They're sending a car for us." Po Po held up her palm for a high five. "Am I good or what?"

Raina patted her grandma's hand. "Good job, Watson. I need to sneak into Sonny's office to grab Ah Gong's journal, too."

"How? They have cameras and guards everywhere, and we're only there for dinner."

"Then we'll have to stay overnight somehow. According to Sonny, no one actually monitors the video in real time. The guards stay in the lawn area by the fence perimeter. And I doubt they walk around in the dark."

Po Po's eyes sparkled. "We can use our ninja outfits."

"Nooo, this time I really need you to get on Kwan Gong's good side. I don't care if you have to put on lingerie and prance around in front of him. If I get caught, Sonny could issue a command to sink me to the bottom of a river. Kwan Gong might be the only one to veto this."

Po Po did a little shimmy with her upper body. The loose skin on her arms didn't stop moving when she did. "Leave this to me. I'll have him wrapped around my pinkie."

Raina laughed. Her grandma—the sexpot. She hoped she wouldn't have to do too much damage control afterward. But what harm could Po Po do to Kwan Gong? It wasn't like the two of them were spring chickens.

They got into the car, and Raina headed toward the apartment. Her grandma pulled out her cell phone and held it up against her ear.

"What the..." Po Po exclaimed. Her voice trailed off.

At the stoplight, Raina glanced at her grandma. "Is everything okay?"

Po Po's eyes were the size of saucers. "What did you tell Matthew about the weekend at the Kwans?"

The light turned green, and Raina returned her attention to the road. She hadn't spoken to Matthew since...

Raina blinked. Wait! "The email. Oh my gosh, I forgot all about the email." She explained to her grandmother the pre-scheduled email for this morning in case something were to happen to her while she was at the Kwans.

"This explains it," Po Po said. "He's on his way to Toronto. He should be here in time for dinner."

RAINA'S STOMACH SANK, squeezing the tuna sandwich into a gurgling knot. What if Matthew got in the way of the investigation? Not intentionally, of course, but he was a homicide detective and would want her to leave things to the professionals. Or worse, what if he teamed up with the local law enforcement to take Sonny down? It would take a far braver woman than she to stand between these two men.

Once inside the rental apartment, Po Po made a

beeline for her bedroom. Raina followed along and flopped on the bed. She couldn't wait to go home. While the furnished apartment was adequate for their needs, it felt like she wore borrowed clothes two sizes too big.

Po Po threw open her closet. "Should we pack an overnight bag?"

"Isn't this a little presumptuous?" Raina asked.

"It's a bit of a drive." Po Po pulled an overnight bag out of the closet. "If one of us drinks a little too much, from the tension of having an ex across the dinner table and a new beau next to her, who could blame her? Why, she might be too drunk to go home."

Raina shook her head. *Please don't let this come to pass.* "We are not bringing Matthew to dinner."

"The man flies across the country to save you. The least you can do is feed him."

Raina wasn't made of ice. What woman didn't melt a little when the man of her dreams rode on a white horse —or a plane—to rescue her? "But I'm not the one feeding. I don't think Sonny would like his love rival sitting across from him at the dinner table. He'll probably want me to go home."

"So what? Sonny can afford to add another seat at the table. And Matthew either comes along for the ride or he can watch from the sidelines. If he can't do either then he's not the right man for you."

"We can't tell him about Ah Gong's journal. He'll want to sneak into the office for us."

"He could do a better job at sneaking than we can. He has plenty of experience working for the Feds."

"But we can do it with style," Raina said. This probably wasn't true, but she didn't want her grandma getting ideas. "Who knows what Sonny and his men would do to Matthew if they caught him? I can't risk it. Better me than him. I can play the bimbo card."

Her grandma gave her a doubtful look. "Rainy, I don't want to bust your bubble, but you're not a good actress."

"I don't need to be good. I just need to convince one person. Did Matthew say what time his flight arrives? I wonder if we have time to get him before the Kwans' driver comes for us."

Po Po pulled her cell phone out of her purse. "He didn't say. Let me text him, so he can get the message you're alive and well once the plane lands." Her grandma tapped on the screen.

Raina went into her bedroom to stuff clean under-wear and a toothbrush into her purse. She logged onto her laptop and wrote an email to Matthew, explaining everything that had happened over the weekend. The time ticked by, but she couldn't get rid of the uneasy feeling in the pit of her stomach. She called Matthew, but the call went straight to voicemail.

She popped back into her grandma's bedroom. "Did Matthew text or call yet? He should have landed by now."

Po Po checked her phone. "Nothing." She dialed his number, listened, and left a message for him to call her back. "He must still have his phone turned off."

Raina went back to the living room, pacing from the window to the door. With his phone off, would Matthew get their messages in time? What if he went straight to the Kwan mansion? With his connections, he could find the address easy enough.

The Kwans's driver came for them at a quarter to four. Raina directed him to swing by the airport before heading to Aurora. As they pulled up to the arrivals curb, she scanned the travelers waiting on the sidewalk with their luggage. No Matthew. She hadn't expected to see him waiting, but she had hoped for a miracle.

Raina leapt out the door. "I'll check inside," she called out over her shoulder and took off.

She raced through the baggage claim area. No tall Chinese man with gold-flecked brown eyes. Her heart raced at the thought of Matthew confronting Sonny. Matthew normally didn't act without meticulous planning, but when it came to her, sometimes he just acted. If anything happened to him...

Raina ran back to the limo, jerked the door open, and threw herself back inside. "To the mansion. As fast as you can," she said to the driver.

Her grandma glanced at her with concern. "Matthew isn't stupid. We'll get there in time to avert any disaster. And you're over-thinking this. He might not even be heading in that direction. Maybe he's looking up friends to get reinforcements before confronting Sonny."

"I hope so," Raina whispered, blinking back tears.

The hour-long drive was a blur. Raina must have dozed off during the drive because the next thing she knew, the driver was standing next to the door and holding it open for her. The vehicle parked next to the steps leading into the mansion.

Her right pinkie itched, and she scratched the little pink bump on it before climbing out. Fantastic. Now she had to deal with hives on top of everything else. She raced up the steps to the mansion.

Cat opened the door, and Raina ran into Freddie Low. He caught her easily before she fell onto the tile floor.

"Whoa!" Freddie said. "Where's the fire?"

"Where is Sonny?" Raina said between gulps of air.

Cat pointed toward the library. "Sonny is in there with a man claiming to be your relative." She raised an eyebrow. "I don't see any family resemblance."

"A relative?" Raina echoed. The knot in her chest eased. Matthew hadn't barged in with guns blazing. Of course, he would have a plan. He didn't wing things.

"Who?" Po Po said from behind Raina.

"Matthew," Raina said.

"He's been part of the family for years," Po Po said, which was technically true. As next door neighbors, Raina and Matthew had grown up together.

"Don't tell me you are planning to leave Sonny at the altar for your cousin," Freddie said with a hint of amusement in his voice.

"What about the altar?" Myling said, stepping out from the house.

"I'll tell you on the way home," Freddie said, guiding his wife toward the car parked in the driveway.

Po Po strolled into the mansion. "Where is Kwan Gong?"

"He's upstairs with Lily," Cat said.

"Tell the men to save some of the drama for dinner. I want to have a show with my wine." Po Po crossed the foyer and headed up the stairs.

Raina stared at her grandma's back. Her grandma wasn't helping her? She blinked. Wait! Was her grandma using her wiles on Kwan Gong? If Raina could stop the men from duking it out until dinner, would she have an ally from the patriarch of the Kwan family?

She took a deep breath. Fine. She could handle things

until then. She strolled toward the library with Cat keeping pace with her.

"If you leave Sonny at the altar, he'll flip out," Cat said. "Last time we had to replace all the furniture in the house."

"I'm sure he can afford it."

"You hurt him, and I'll have to hurt you."

Raina stopped and swung to face the other woman. "This is none of your business." She was taking her anxiety out on Cat, but she couldn't stop herself. "I'm here as a favor to Sonny."

Cat ran a finger along the gun handle hidden underneath the shrug she wore over her red tank top. Her red leather completed the look. "I'm the Nine Dragons Enforcer. When it comes to protecting Kwans, it's my business."

"Oh, like how you're protecting Lily?" Raina asked. Did the woman only wear mono color?

Cat stiffened. "What the fu—"

"What is going on here?" Sonny called out.

Raina spun around to find both Sonny and Matthew coming out of the library. Her heart stopped for half a breath and sped up at the familiar broad shoulders and tousled black hair. Her knight came to rescue her with nothing more than a gym-size carry-on bag.

12

THE FALLOUT

Matthew's gold-flecked brown eyes caught hers. The tension around his eyes disappeared. The white-knuckled grip on the handle of his carry-on bag loosened. He didn't smile—as a matter of fact, he was scowling like he caught sight of an errant family member—but Raina knew he was relieved to find her alive and in one piece. She gave him a Miss America wave. It wouldn't save her from a lecture, but it was a small price for the new white hairs on his head.

The two men sauntered over—two frozen peas from the same bag. Tall, well-muscled, and surrounded with a layer of hard ice. And yet, once they thawed, there was a soft mushy side. Neither man would be happy with this assessment.

"Did you get my message?" Raina asked Matthew.

"No, my phone ran out of juice," Matthew said. "I heard congratulations are in order."

Sonny slung an arm across Raina's shoulders. "I still can't believe she said yes."

Raina stiffened, but she didn't shrug off his arm. What game was Sonny playing? Since he kept tabs on her, he knew perfectly well who Matthew was and what he meant to her.

Matthew glanced at her hand. "Since you didn't put a ring on her, she's still a free agent."

"We haven't gotten a chance to go shopping," Sonny said, smiling and stretching the scar on the side of his face.

Matthew held Raina's gaze. He reached into his pocket and pulled out a half-carat diamond ring on a platinum band. The same one he had given her during their brief twenty-four-hour marriage in Las Vegas. He'd added rubies to either side of the diamond since the last time she'd seen the ring—three weeks ago.

"How about this one?" Matthew said. "The rubies belonged to Raina's other grandma."

Raina couldn't breathe, and her heart thumped painfully against her chest. The ring threw off sparks and danger. By "other grandma," he meant his grandma, who was Po Po's best friend. She swallowed the lump in her throat. He'd meant the proposal this time. He slipped it on her finger before she could react.

Her fingers curled protectively around the ring. Did he just propose to her again? In front of Sonny and Cat? Did she say yes? She should take this ring off. She should hand it—

Sonny's hand tightened on her shoulder. "You don't want an old ring, do you, Rainy? I'll take you shopping tomorrow."

Raina glanced at Sonny, blinking away her dilemma with Matthew. This wasn't the time or place for them to discuss their relationship. Sonny knew shopping for rings wasn't part of their bargain. "I know it's rude, but I hope you don't mind adding my cousin to your dinner table."

"It's not a problem. Cat, go tell the cook," Sonny said. He didn't even glance at his second in command.

Cat opened her mouth to protest, huffed, and trotted toward the kitchen downstairs. The two men stared at each other, ignoring Raina. She shifted her weight from foot to foot at the silence.

Kwan Gong came down the stairs half a heartbeat later to welcome them. Po Po clung to his arm, batting her eyes at him whenever he glanced at her. With her cone-shaped breasts and pimp cane, her grandma didn't quite get the message she didn't fit the image of a matron or sex goddess.

Matthew stared at her grandmother's outfit, but his expression gave nothing away. Raina bit her lower lip to keep from giggling. Well, if he wanted in on the family this badly, he would have to learn to roll with her grandma's eccentricity.

"Are we ready to eat?" Kwan Gong said, flashing the dentures in his mouth. He led the way into a smaller dining room. Her grandma sashayed next to him, or at least Raina assumed the swinging gait was a sashay.

Sonny followed his grandfather, tugging Raina along with Matthew following in their rear. The servants came in with several courses, and at one point, Cat slipped onto a chair and ate like she hadn't been MIA for the last half an hour. No one seemed to care that Lily Kwan was still hiding out in her bedroom.

"So you are Raina's cousin?" Kwan Gong asked Matthew, setting his fork down.

"Yes, from the Sun side of the family," Matthew answered. His voice was steady and even. He was definitely a much better liar than Raina.

"Getting engaged to your cousin is the smartest thing my grandson ever did."

Matthew flicked a glance at Raina and returned to cutting his steak. "Good luck with that. Raina and I were once married for less than forty-eight hours."

Po Po choked mid-sip on her wine, spraying droplets across the table.

Sonny jerked back on his chair but not before getting his face splattered. He grimaced as he wiped at it with a napkin.

"Married?" Kwan Gong swirled his head between Raina and Matthew. "I thought the two of you are related." The amusement left his face.

"I said we're related by marriage." Matthew nodded at Raina's direction. "She's still wearing the ring I gave her."

Raina groaned inwardly at the twinkle in his eyes. She leaned back into her chair, hoping to disappear from the room.

Kwan Gong rose from his chair and pointed a finger at his grandson. "Is this some kind of joke? This is the last straw, Sonny. You killed your brother, and now you're bringing a slut home!"

Po Po jerked away from him like he slapped her. "Who are you—"

Sonny threw his hands up in the air. "We're not even engaged. I only put on this dog and pony show for Myling—"

Kwan Gong's face turned into a shade of eggplant. "You should have married her—"

"And always be compared to my brother? I don't want a marriage like Jerry's."

"We needed an alliance with Lily's family—"

"Fu—"

"You spoiled, ungrateful brat! It's your duty to strengthen the Nine Dragons—"

Sonny jabbed a finger at the scar on this face. "I have already done my duty for the triad. I didn't ask for this life."

"But you sure enjoyed the money and power though." By this time Kwan Gong's body quivered and swayed. "You can't have it without sacrifice."

Sonny glared at his grandfather. His chest heaved with suppressed emotions.

The room was dead quiet except for the heavy breathing from the Kwan men. Raina's wide eyes met her grandma's. Neither had bargained for this kind of dinner show. Po Po was shocked into silence for once. Matthew's expression was stony, and he tightened his grip on the steak knife. Surprisingly, Cat continued to eat like this happened at every meal.

Sonny gasped. His breath came out in a sharp swish and caught Raina's attention. She glanced over in time to see his expression change from anger to confusion and fear. She followed his gaze and saw Kwan Gong clutching his chest. His forehead was covered in the sheen of sweat. He dropped onto his chair, and his head fell on Po Po's lap.

Her grandma cradled Kwan Gong's head automatically. "I don't know how to help him." Her voice came out several decibels higher than normal.

Sonny leapt from his chair. It crashed onto the floor

when he ran to his grandfather's side. He searched his pockets and pulled out a medicine bottle. His hands shook, but he managed to open the childproof cap. He grabbed his grandfather's chin and popped the white pill into his mouth.

"We need an ambulance. Give me your phone," Matthew said. His voice sounded calm, but Raina knew he was worried by the way he kept perfectly still.

Raina pulled out her new cell phone from her purse and handed it over. Was the elderly man having a heart attack? She prayed this wasn't the case. The Kwan family didn't need another death.

Cat froze in her chair with the fork suspended midway to her mouth. The henchwoman was clearly useless in an emergency that didn't require a gun.

The medication kicked in, and Kwan Gong's face lost its pinched, ashen look. Po Po wiped the sweat off his face with a napkin.

The ambulance arrived and checked out Kwan Gong. Her grandma ended up with a bruise on her thigh and had to use the pimp cane to get up from the chair. Sonny insisted his grandfather go to the hospital for a more thorough examination. Kwan Gong didn't even protest and asked Po Po to keep him company.

Sonny watched the ambulance drive away from the front door. "I can't believe he'd rather have your grandma with him than me."

Raina patted his shoulder. "It's not you. People just love my grandma. Do you want me to drive you to the hospital? You should be there."

He glanced down at her, covering her hand with his. "The chauffeur can do it. You might as well get some sleep until your grandma comes back. Just ask the house-keeper for a couple guest rooms."

Raina nodded. She would have the run of the mansion with both Sonny and Kwan Gong at the hospital. She lowered her eyes so he didn't see the excitement in them. Sneaking into his office had just gotten easier. "I'll tell Lily what happened."

Sonny left a few minutes later, and Raina found herself alone with Matthew for the first time.

WHEN RAINA RETURNED to the dining room, the servants were clearing away the last of the dishes. She peeked into several living rooms—or maybe the correct term was sitting rooms—but didn't see Matthew or Cat.

The mansion was too big to go looking for them room by room. Besides, did she really want to be alone with Matthew right now? She wasn't ready for the lecture anyway. This was the perfect time to have a little chat with Lily Kwan though.

Raina headed downstairs toward the servants' work-rooms to look for the housekeeper. When she found the lady, the housekeeper showed her to the door of Lily's bedroom suite and left. Raina knocked, but there was no answer.

"Lily? This is Raina Sun, Sonny's, uh"—now that the truth was out, there was no point in pretending —"friend. I want to make sure you're okay," Raina said to the door.

No answer.

Raina knocked again. *Tap. Tap. Tap.*

"What are you doing here?" Cat called out from behind her.

Raina spun around. The Nine Dragons Enforcer looked even fiercer today with her blood-red clothing. The rich chestnut hair was pulled back into a side braid with a red ribbon woven through it. Raina couldn't tell if Cat disliked her because of her role in the recent events, or if Cat took a personal dislike to her.

"I'm concerned about Lily. No one has seen her in the last two days. Don't you find this strange? Even if she had food hidden in her bedroom suite, she would have run out by now," Raina said.

"She's probably grieving," Cat said.

Raina couldn't believe Cat said the statement with a straight face. She was truly a much better actress than Raina was. "Lily might not be dancing on her husband's grave, but she's not grieving. Before Jerry's death, weren't you two planning to run off into the sunset together?"

Cat raised an eyebrow. "Why would I run off with Lily?"

"Aren't the two of you lovers?" As soon as the question left her mouth, Raina felt ridiculous. She blamed it on her grandma's influence.

Cat studied Raina, weighing her intentions. "I was trying to help Lily leave the family. If Kwan Gong found out about our hare-brained scheme, he would put me back into the life Jerry had rescued me from."

Raina glanced around the hall. There was only the two of them. She didn't have to ask what life Cat meant. The way she said it, it could only mean one thing—human trafficking. But Jerry didn't seem like the type to help a woman without strings. "Why are you helping her? Why risk losing your position in the organization?"

"If you laugh"—Cat's hand reached for the gun in her shoulder holster before she caught herself in time. She cleared her throat, pretending like nothing had happened.

Raina shook her head and hoped her expression invited the confidence. They were on the brink of a breakthrough in the murder investigation, and she didn't want to blow it. She crossed her fingers behind her back.

"Jerry would take his frustrations out on Lily, both verbally and physically. If I could save her then maybe I can save myself. She said she'd take me with her," Cat said, her eyes focused on something far away.

"Why do you care about Lily? Jerry saved you. Shouldn't your loyalty lie with him?"

"I already paid my dues." Cat's tone was curt. "I'm glad he's dead."

Raina licked her lower lip. It was none of her business how Cat paid her dues, but she might have had her own reasons for wanting Jerry dead. "Why were you helping Lily escape? You don't seem like the type to have a Louis Vuitton overnight bag?"

"Because I can't afford it?"

"No, you're more of a Kate Spade girl." Actually, Raina hadn't given it much thought, but the brighter patterns and more youthful designs would match Cat's style. She smiled inwardly. After spending a lifetime with her mom and older sister—the shopaholics in the family—Raina actually knew the difference between the two brands.

"The men either ignore me or want to bed me. The women are no better, making catty comments behind my back." Cat was quiet for a moment. "Frankly, I don't care who killed Jerry, but if I could help Sonny, I would."

"Sonny?" Raina echoed. Now this would be news to Sonny. Could Cat have killed Jerry to help Sonny secure his position in the organization after all? "Did you kill Jerry?"

"No."

"What about Lily? Could she have killed her husband?"

"Why don't you ask her yourself?" Cat knocked on the bedroom door.

The door opened in a slow arc. No one was on the other side. Raina and Cat looked at each other. In that one heartbeat, Cat pulled out her gun and shifted in front of Raina.

They crept into the room. Cat two-fisted the gun and hunched as if she was expecting a shoot-out. Raina let the henchwoman lead the way. She figured whoever had gotten past security would take more than the two of them to take down. And since she couldn't back away, whatever happened would happen. She pulled her grandma's hair stick from her purse and held it in front of her like a knife.

The bedroom suite looked like a fancy hotel room with curtains and bedspread in the same shade of gray-blue and dark wood furniture. A few personal items were scattered around the suite. How depressing! Lily's sanctuary looked identical to the guest suite.

It took less than a minute to search the bedroom suite. Lily was nowhere to be found and neither was the Louis Vuitton overnight bag.

13

CHASING FATE

Raina put the hair stick back into her purse. She spun around and surveyed the bedroom. There was no sign of a struggle. Lily had flown the coop. At this point, would the Kwan men care?

"Do you know anything about this?" Raina asked.

Cat shook her head. "How did she leave the property without anyone noticing? It's not like she can sneak out on the back of someone's truck."

"Maybe she hasn't left the property yet. Should we search for her?"

"You can, if you want. I am heading back to my house."

"You don't stay here?"

"I'd rather sleep in my own bed."

Raina raised an eyebrow. "Don't you care what happened to Lily?"

"She caught me at a moment of weakness, and I don't weasel my way out of a promise. But as far as I'm concerned, our deal dissolved on the night her husband died."

Cat left shortly afterward, and Raina headed downstairs to the staff area to find the head housekeeper again. Should she raise the alarm about Lily? If she had nothing to do with the death, Raina didn't want to be the one to trap her here. She was halfway down the stairs to the first floor when a sudden thought struck her. Could she use Lily's disappearance as an excuse to check the surveillance video in Sonny's office?

Raina smiled. Yes, Lily's disappearance would be the perfect distraction. First, she would have to alert the staff to start a search party. She almost skipped her way into the kitchen but caught herself in the last minute in front of the panel covering the entrance to the downstairs kitchen.

She got rid of her smile and put on a frown before trotting down the stairs. There was no one in sight. The lights were on a lower setting, creating a dim tunnel effect in the staff hallway. She checked the time on her cell phone. It was close to ten o'clock. Even if the staff didn't live on the premises, surely one person must be at the Kwan's beck and call 24/7. Maybe the head housekeeper?

Raina's footsteps echoed around her. "Hello? Anyone here?" As soon as the words left her mouth, a sense of unease settled into the pit of her stomach. This was how the slasher movies began...in an empty, spooky mansion.

A hand grabbed her elbow. Raina jumped and screamed. A flash of adrenaline shot through her, and she brought her elbow up to ram it into her attacker.

A familiar voice said, "Rainy, it's me." Matthew's aftershave—a clean water and sage scent—hit her a second too late. She could have broken his nose.

Raina's heartbeat pounded in her ears. She jerked her arm and spun around. "I almost peed in my pants."

"That's still better than the heart attack you gave me with your email."

"I'm sorry," Raina whispered. She felt a twinge of guilt for talking about a heart attack when Kwan Gong was at the hospital but dismissed the thought just as quickly. She didn't have the time or the mental energy to think about him.

"What are you doing, skulking around the mansion?"

"I'm not skulking. Where have you been?"

One corner of Matthew's lips curled. "Skulking. It's not every day I get invited to a triad's base of operation."

"You're not here on official duty. And it's not in your jurisdiction." Raina's tone came out harsher than she intended. For some crazy reason, she wanted to protect Sonny. Probably because he trusted her.

"You sound like you are enamored with Sonny Kwan's lifestyle." Matthew's tone held a hint of disapproval.

"Of course not. But we are guests in his home, and he trusts us enough to leave us here while the family is at the hospital. It would be rude for us to—" Raina broke off. The irony was not lost on her. She changed her tactic and softened her tone. "Why don't you get some rest? I'm sure you're exhausted from flying across the country."

"Why do I have the feeling you're trying to get rid me?"

"I'm always trying to get rid of you. You just keep coming back." Raina meant all those times they had gotten together in the last decade since high school.

"Now, have you seen the head housekeeper? No one has seen Lily Kwan in two days, and now she has disappeared from the mansion."

"I cross mountains and rivers to rescue my girl. And this is what I get? I don't think so."

Matthew pulled Raina into a familiar embrace, his arms wrapping around her back and hip. She could have struggled, but she was tired of fighting the inevitable. She placed her hand on his bicep, the ring sparkling with an inner fire in the dim light, and stood on tippy toes for the kiss.

According to an old Chinese saying, in their previous lives, their bones must have gotten mixed up in the same grave. This was the only explanation for the connection between them, and why they couldn't let each other go. If it was fate, then Raina would surrender to it.

The kiss only lasted a minute, but it shifted something between them. Raina saw it in his eyes and heard it in his sigh. They were silent for several long minutes. And she enjoyed the feel of his arms around her again.

"You want to tell me what's going on here?" Matthew finally asked.

Raina filled him in on Jerry's death and Lily's disappearance.

"All this for your grandfather's journal?" he asked. "Your grandma is lucky to have you."

She smiled. "No, I'm lucky to have her. So how do I start a search party without the staff?"

"The head housekeeper is in her office down the hall."

He released her, and she felt a quick flash of regret. If only they had more time to themselves.

ONCE THEY FOUND the head housekeeper, she called the guard shack. The security team would search the grounds outside while the head housekeeper and Matthew would start the search inside the mansion. Raina would catch up with them once she finished her call to her grandma.

She told her grandma about Lily's disappearance from the mansion. "Now that everyone is busy looking for Lily, I'm going in."

"Make it quick. We're leaving in the next few minutes. The hospital is less than fifteen minutes from the mansion."

"Can't you make Sonny stop somewhere on the way back? What about the drive-thru?"

"I'll try my best. Just hurry."

Raina hung up and slipped the phone back into her purse. She pulled a hair stick out and headed toward Sonny's office. She stepped outside into the courtyard and stood still until her eyes adjusted to the dim moonlight.

She didn't dare use the light from the hair stick until she was inside the office. The security team might come to check out the light, thinking it was Lily.

Raina was halfway across the courtyard when the hair on the back of her neck stiffened. She paused, cocking her head to listen. Her heartbeat roared inside her ears. Geez, she couldn't hear a thing.

She squinted into the darkness. Was it her imagination playing tricks on her or did she hear something? The dim moonlight exaggerated the shadows. She was about to move, when she heard the shuffling noise again. There! Soft footsteps approached her from the direction of Sonny's office.

What the heck? Who would be coming toward her? The person would bump into her in a minute if she didn't move out of the way. She shifted, but not quick enough.

Kaboom!

Hot and thick air rushed at Raina's face, and the sky lit up with fire. The person in front of Raina slammed into her, and the momentum carried her back several inches before the two of them fell on top of each other onto the pavers on the floor.

Raina fell on her hip, and a sharp pain ran down her leg. She screamed, but the noise got lost as another explosion from Sonny's office blasted through the air. Soot and debris rained down on her.

She threw her hands over her head and stayed on the ground. Her ears rang and soot clogged her throat. The dark shape moaned and moved, untangling herself from Raina's legs. By the glow of the flames, she could tell the person was a woman by her smaller frame. The woman struggled to her feet, swaying and moaning.

A door slammed open from the direction of the mansion. A beam of light swept across the courtyard until it landed on Raina. Footsteps ran toward her.

Gentle hands brushed a curl from Raina's cheek. Matthew! His mouth moved, but she couldn't hear anything beyond the ringing in her ears. She blinked, or at least she thought she did, but the next thing she knew he was shaking her shoulder.

He yelled something at her again, gesturing toward

the mansion. His eyes were calm in the flickering flame. He probably wanted to move her but was afraid to.

"I'm fine," she croaked.

He said something to her again. Over his shoulder, she saw glimpses of the head housekeeper tending to the other woman in the courtyard.

Raina cupped a hand behind her ear and shook her head. He probably didn't hear her. She pushed herself off the ground with shaking arms, hoping he would interpret this correctly. She wasn't going anywhere without his help.

He did. He scooped her into his arms and ran toward the mansion. Raina's head bounced off his firm chest. Her gritty eyelids slid closed and she blanked out for the next few seconds.

When he shook her again, she was on a corner chair in the kitchen, leaning against the wall with Matthew kneeling in front of her.

Raina's gaze lingered on his beautiful face. He said something and gestured at the direction of the courtyard. She nodded. "Go. I'm fine."

Matthew kissed her on the forehead and wiped the dark soot off his lips. When he disappeared from her sight, she felt a moment of panic. Her breaths came out in sharp, jagged puffs. What if there was another bomb in Sonny's office? What if this was the last time she'd see him?

Her gaze rolled around the kitchen. She wasn't going to pass out. She wasn't going to be that girl who fainted because her man ran into a dangerous situation. She couldn't breathe. Her chest was moving rapidly, but she wasn't getting air.

Someone moved into her line of sight. The head housekeeper held a yellow dishtowel to Lily's bleeding face. So that was the other woman in the courtyard. The room became a blinding white light, and she squinted to keep the other two women in focus.

"You'll need a different towel soon," Raina croaked as the blood soaked through the yellow fabric.

Her eyes slid closed. There was a second of freefall, and she felt the impact of her body hitting the floor. She was too far gone to even make a peep. Not that she would have heard it.

14

BEAUTIFUL EYEBROWS

When Raina returned to the land of the living, she was lying on something softer than the floor. Her hip throbbed, but that was to be expected. She wiggled her toes. Everything seemed to be in working order. Too bad she had to faint like a wimp at the sight of blood.

Despite the faint ringing in her ears, she caught snatches of Matthew's conversation with someone. Cracking open one eyelid, a powder blue wall came into focus. She was in the small sitting room where she'd served tea to the police. She closed her eye again to eavesdrop on the conversation.

"...death from anaphylaxis..."

"...accidental?"

"Unlikely...family is careful..."

Raina felt a flash of satisfaction. Matthew was chatting with Detective Bibb about Jerry's death. She suspected the murderer had used Jerry's allergies against him. Now here was the official confirmation. Not that the police would listen to an amateur like her. No, she wasn't bitter.

"...help...."

"...Kwan...insider..."

Someone cleared his throat. The conversation ceased, and there was a moment of silence. Did they suspect she was awake? Why didn't Matthew re-engage the detective to pry more information from him?

From behind her eyelids, she could sense a shift in the light. Someone peering down at her? Brisk footsteps left the room. Great. There went her chance to get official information on the murder investigation.

Raina wanted to groan out loud. Matthew could be so by the books sometimes. Did she want to open her eyes and face his wrath? It wasn't like she could pretend to be unconscious forever. Maybe if she used her charm to soften him up... She opened her eyes slowly, blinking dreamily, up at...Detective Bibb?

Her gaze swept the room. Where was Matthew?

"Welcome back, Miss Sun," Detective Bibb said.

Raina blinked again, trying to buy a moment to think. Why would Matthew leave her unprotected with the detective? "I have a head injury. I can't take questions right now."

"The paramedics just arrived. Your other fiancé will bring them in to check on you after they take a look at Lily Kwan," Detective Bibb said. "You seem to have a knack for collecting fiancés like some women collect shoes."

Raina put the back of her hand to her forehead. "My head..." she mumbled, hoping her voice sounded feeble and weak. She didn't have to try too hard. The last few hours had sapped her energy more than she realized.

"Okay." Detective Bibb headed toward the door. "We can always do this after the paramedics find nothing wrong with you. The station is more conducive to an interrogation anyway."

Raina sat up on the sofa. The room tilted, and she held onto the armrest. She should move slower. Throwing up at the detective's feet wouldn't help the situation. "Fine! Let's just get this over with."

Detective Bibb paused at the doorway. "Are you sure? I wouldn't want to tax you. A head wound is no laughing matter."

"I said I'm fine," Raina said through gritted teeth.

The detective sat down on the armchair next to the sofa and pulled out his notebook. "So does Sonny Kwan know you have another fiancé waiting in the wings?"

"My relationship with Sonny is none of your concern."

"I like Matthew Louie. A straight shooter. One of the good guys keeping people like Sonny Kwan off the streets. I'd hate to see you hurt him."

"Really, Detective? You're giving me dating advice?"

He ignored her comment. "What were you and Lily Kwan doing in the courtyard before the explosions?"

"I don't know what she was doing. No one had seen her in two days, and when she disappeared from her room, we organized a search party."

"This still doesn't explain why you were near Sonny's office when it exploded."

"How do you know it's Sonny's office?"

Detective Bibb ignored her question. "What were you

hoping to find in there? Or did you put the bombs in there?"

Raina pointed to her face. The skin still felt tight and raw. She hadn't seen it yet, but it wouldn't be a pretty sight. "You think I would do this to myself?"

He ignored her question again. "Why were you near Sonny's office?"

Raina took a deep breath. She felt a strong desire to stab him on the thigh with her grandma's hair stick. Not because she wanted to hurt him, but because she was frustrated, and he was...doing his job.

Her late grandfather's journal just went up in flames, along with her grandma's peace of mind. Everything she had done in the last few months had been for naught.

She blinked at the burning tears in her eyes. To come this close...only to lose it in an explosion. A stupid explosion that came out of the blue. Her lower lip wobbled, and a tear rolled down her face.

Detective Bibb narrowed his eyes, scowling. "Enough of that. Tears will just delay the questions."

"I know," Raina croaked. She covered her face with her hands. She would not break down. She swiped at another tear.

Why did her life have a habit of imploding? She wasn't a bad person. If she had known this would happen, she wouldn't have gotten involved with Sonny in the first place. Her chest tightened and a whimper escaped from her lips before she could stop herself. She felt so stupid. So amazingly naive. So—

"Hey, you just lived through an explosion. You should go buy a lottery ticket," Detective Bibb said gruffly. He pulled a wrinkled handkerchief out of his pocket and gestured for her to take it.

The filthy cloth did her in. Raina covered her face and sobbed. Her heart ached from the loss of the journal and the post-adrenaline surge. She wanted nothing more than to curl up in the guest bed and have a good cry.

"What happened?" Matthew asked, his voice brisk and commanding. He rushed into the room and wrapped his arms around Raina. "Is she done here, Detective?"

"Get some rest, Ms. Sun," Detective Bibb said, closing his notebook. "We'll have a chat after you get a chance to calm down. We have evidence that indicates there was someone else in the alcove on the night Jerry died."

MATTHEW WRAPPED an arm around Raina's waist and helped her out into the foyer. Detective Bibb was a mere step behind them. He strode off toward Sonny's office without a backward glance. Two paramedics rolled a gurney from the downstairs staff area—there must be an elevator somewhere—toward the main door.

Raina was still reeling from what Detective Bibb said. He must know she'd lied on the night of the birthday party. Why did he tell her what he knew? Was it to throw off her equilibrium? Or did he want to see how she would react? If he thought she would break down and blabber, then he had a long wait coming.

She wiped the tears from her face. There would be time for tears later. She glanced up at Matthew. "I want to talk to Lily."

Matthew kissed her on the side of her head. "I can see someone is feeling better already."

He guided them toward the paramedics. As he spoke quietly with the technicians, Raina stepped up to the gurney. The paramedics had removed the dish towel and bandaged the cut on Lily's head, but blood was already seeping through. The cut would probably require stitches. They were both lucky to still be alive.

"How are you feeling?" Raina asked Lily.

"Stupid. I should have known Sonny wouldn't leave evidence lying around in his office without a kill switch," Lily said.

Raina studied the other woman. Would Sonny really rig his office with bombs? But if she didn't put the bombs in there, then who did? "How did you trigger the bomb?"

"I don't know. Maybe I punched in too many combinations on the keypad. I was lucky to leave when I did." Lily shuddered. "I don't even want to think about what could have happened if the bomb went off when I was still at the keypad."

"What were you doing at Sonny's office in the first place?"

"I could ask you the same thing," Lily said.

"I was looking for you. We organized a search party. I wanted to check the video feed to see if you were still on the property. I was concerned about you." The lies rolled smoothly out of Raina's mouth.

Lily studied her for a long moment. "I was looking for an insurance policy. Even though Jerry is dead, I need a guarantee that the Kwan family will let me go."

"What about your father? Couldn't he protect you?"

Lily snorted. "He's just as bad as the Kwans. I should have run away, but where could I go? He controls the underground network in Thailand. I thought I could make it work with Jerry." She gestured at her surroundings. "This isn't such a bad life. But Jerry resented me from the moment he laid eyes on me. I even turned a blind eye when he took up a mistress, but that was not enough for him."

"Did you have Jerry's EpiPen on the night he died?"

"Yes, he kept it in my purse. I called him several times that night, but he was probably dead by then."

Raina licked her lips. The question had to be asked. "Do you know who his mis—"

"Let's check you out," the paramedic said, cutting Raina off.

"Give me a minute," Raina said.

"Now. We need to get her to the hospital," he said, indicating Lily.

He guided Raina a few feet away to give them some semblance of privacy. He took her blood pressure, checked her eyes, and asked several questions about how she was feeling. "You're fine. If you feel any worse, you could call your doctor in the morning."

When Raina joined Lily again, she had dozed off on the gurney. The paramedics wheeled Lily toward the ambulance waiting in the driveway. Raina and Matthew watched until the ambulance was no longer in sight. When they went back into the foyer, the head house-keeper was waiting for them.

"Miss Sun," the head housekeeper said, wringing her hands.

"Yes?" Raina said.

The head housekeeper pulled an envelope from her pocket.

Raina automatically reached for it.

"Please give this to Mr. Kwan. I quit." The head house-keeper spun on her heels and left.

"Can this day get any worse?" Raina asked.

Matthew slung an arm around Raina's shoulders. "Look on the bright side, Rainy. You still got both your eyebrows. Not many people can walk away from an explosion and say that."

15

STAR-CROSSED LOVERS

When Raina woke the next morning, she found a note next to her pillow. Matthew had left to have coffee with the detective in town. She glanced at the display on her cell phone. It was seven in the morning. She had less than five hours of sleep last night.

She stared at the canopy above the bed, not really looking at it. Why did these things always happen to her? Without the journal, why was she still here? She should pack up, grab her grandma, and head back to their uneventful life at Gold Springs. Matthew could take care of himself.

She sighed, and her thoughts shifted gear. Who would blow up Sonny's office? The man probably had enemies up the wazoo, but they wouldn't have made it past the guard patrolling the property. Not unless they were family or...

Raina's eyes widened. The Lows! How could she have forgotten about them? They were on their way out when

Raina arrived yesterday. With the two of them, it would be easy for one of them to distract Sonny while the other planted the bombs. She could see Myling using her wiles on her ex.

But why? They needed Sonny to help take care of the Italian mob. Or did they? Who had verified this? Surely Sonny would send out scouts to investigate this before committing the Nine Dragons. She must ask Sonny or Cat the next time she saw either of them.

She went to the restroom to do her business. When she washed her hands, she studied her reflection in the mirror for the first time since the explosion. Her skin was red like she fell asleep next to the pool without sunblock. She swallowed at the thought of what could have happened. Yep, Matthew was right. At least she still had her eyebrows.

While Raina might have lost her grandfather's journal, all was not yet lost. Sonny had read the journal. She could still access its secrets if she played her cards right with Sonny. If she found out who killed his brother, Sonny would have to tell her why her grandfather sought and married this mysterious woman in China when he was engaged to her grandma at the time.

Raina left the bedroom suite and headed toward the downstairs staff area. She passed a maid heading upstairs, holding a bucket and mop. Who supervised the staff work now that the head housekeeper and Lily were both out of the picture? The role certainly didn't fall on her now that she was no longer "engaged" to Sonny.

She strolled through the servants hall and pushed open the side door to the courtyard. She sucked in her breath at the sight before her. The English cottage had dark scorched marks crawling on its once light and airy stonework like an infestation. The roof caved in on itself and all the windows were blown out. Debris surrounded the building like the half-burnt joss paper a careless daughter-in-law would toss on an ancestor's tomb.

While Raina's footsteps crunched on the glass, her gaze scanned the debris, searching for the journal's distinctive Chinese longevity symbol. She didn't think it would survive the explosion, but stranger things had happened before.

From the corners of her eyes, Raina saw movement in the shadow of the courtyard wall. She shifted her gaze to find Sonny with one leg propped against the brick wall and his face turned up to the sky. She squinted. Were those tears on his face? She took a step toward him, and he brushed a hand across his cheek.

Sonny stepped away from the wall. He strode toward her with the measured steps of a predator stalking its prey. "It's about time you showed your face."

Raina jerked at the sound of his voice. Her mouth went dry, and she stiffened her spine to reinforce her trembling legs. Yikes! What if he thought she had something to do with the explosion?

"How...how is Kwan Gong?" Raina asked, ignoring the hostility rolling off of him.

He invaded her personal space, stopping a foot away from her. "No thanks to your boyfriend, my grandfather is still at the hospital," he spat.

"You were the one to bait Matthew in the first place," she said. "Is my grandma still at his bedside?" It wouldn't hurt to remind him of their family connection. Surely he wouldn't bind and throw an old family friend into the river?

Sonny studied her, and she obliged him by tilting her head and giving him her best wide-eyed innocent look. The tightness around his eyes eased, but he continued to scowl at her.

"I left you in charge last night. And I come home to this?" His hand swept at the ruined cottage.

Raina shifted from foot to foot. "I...I..." He didn't have to put it that way. It wasn't her fault. The bomb would have exploded whether or not she was in the courtyard. And what was this business about being in charge? "I'm sorry, but I didn't put the bomb in your office." She explained what happened with Lily and how she thought the video feed might help the search party.

"And just how were you planning to get into the office without the key code?"

"Kept punching in numbers until I got a green light? I don't know. I didn't really have a plan."

Sonny raised an eyebrow. "Are you sure this was your only intent? I would have taken advantage of the situation and snooped around the office."

"I don't snoop. I was trying to be helpful." Raina's mood shifted, and she glanced at the ruined cottage. "Was my late grandfather's journal inside your office?" She knew the answer to her question, but she hoped he might have moved it.

"Yes, it was in there."

As they surveyed the scene before them, they were silent for several moments, lost in their own thoughts. Raina sighed. She couldn't walk away from this murder investigation now. She had to see this through so Sonny would tell her everything he knew about her grandfather's past. If she had a choice, this wouldn't be her first.

"Who do you think—" Raina started.

"You're the only person I trust—" Sonny broke off.

They both stopped and regarded each other. Sonny gestured for her to continue, but Raina hesitated. She wanted to hear what he had to say first to gauge how he would take the suggestion that his ex might have blown up his office.

Okay, technically it could be either Myling or Freddie. They both had the opportunity to plant the bombs in Sonny's office while they were here yesterday. And because they were married to each other, there was the possibility the two of them were in it together. Or it could still be Cat.

Raina had no idea why the Lows or Cat would be interested in Sonny's office. Did everyone know he kept the video recordings in his office? "You first."

Sonny raked a hand through his hair, making the ends stand out in agitation. "I don't know who I can trust anymore. The bomb exploded from the inside of my office. This clears you." He studied her until she broke the eye contact. "I think I can trust you. I want to trust you."

"I'm not interested in your business. With my grandfather's journal up in smoke, you have the information I need. We have a bargain, and I expect you to honor it."

"I guess this is the best I can expect."

"I'm sorry about what happened to your brother."

"With my grandfather busy building his empire, my brother looked out for me. We used to play here when we were kids. Now I'm the only one left..." His voice cracked at the end. He turned his face away from her and cleared his throat. "I will tell you everything I know once we solve my brother's murder."

Raina believed him. There was no way he could fake the pain in his voice. "With Lily in the hospital, this eliminates her as a suspect."

"This is assuming she's smart enough to not explode the bombs before she got away from the scene."

"Let's assume she's smart enough." Raina had seen the look on Lily's face in the kitchen after the explosion. She had no idea what hit her. "This leaves Cat and the Lows. Do you think the explosion is connected to your brother's death?"

"I don't know. Cat and Myling wouldn't hurt Jerry, though I'm not so sure about Freddie."

"I know Jerry saved Cat, but Myling? Her engagement to you didn't mean she couldn't have a deep resentment toward Jerry." Raina shrugged. "She could be a hired assassin."

Sonny chuckled and when he caught sight of her confusion, it turned into a full belly laugh.

Raina folded her arms across her chest. "I don't see what's so funny."

"Myling grew up in this house with my brother and me. Kwan Gong didn't know this, but Myling and Jerry were lovers all through high school."

RAINA'S JAW DROPPED. Could this be the source of animosity between the Kwan brothers? She had assumed it was the Dai Lo position that caused the rift between the brothers. But what if Jerry were still in love with Myling? "When did they stop—"

Sonny's phone rang, cutting her off. He pulled the phone from his pocket and glanced at the display. "I have to take this. It's from the police."

He turned away from her and tapped on the screen. "Hello?" He strolled away from her to take his call.

Raina's mind raced with what he told her. She studied his muscled back. Maybe Sonny had been telling the truth. Maybe he was over Myling because he had never been in love with her in the first place. The Sonny-Myling-Jerry triangle was too confusing. She needed some facts, not more speculation.

However, the relationship between Myling and the Kwan brothers gave Freddie Low the perfect excuse for murder. What man wanted to believe he had been second-best, or third-best in this case, all along?

Footsteps approached the courtyard. Raina spun around and saw Matthew heading toward them. Uh-oh. This could only mean trouble. She couldn't have the two men sniping at each other when she was almost at a breakthrough with Sonny.

Raina trotted toward Matthew, hoping to deter him before Sonny got off the phone. "I can't talk right now. Can we catch up in about half an hour?"

"I bring you news from the police station, and this is my reception?" Matthew asked. His eyes twinkled, flashing golden flecks in the sunlight.

Raina glanced over her shoulder. "I think Sonny is on the verge of telling me something important that could be vital to the murder investigation. You're kinda killing the mood by being here."

"Uh!" Matthew clapped his hands to his heart like she had stabbed him. "How do you know the intel I have isn't the final clue you're looking for, old wise one?"

Raina slapped him playfully on his arm. "Will you quit it? This is serious."

"Hon, if you can't joke about death, you'll end up crying about it. Now move along. My business here is with Sonny."

"What?" she asked.

"Louie," Sonny said from behind Raina.

Matthew did the manly chin tip men used to greet each other. "Is this a good time?"

Sonny nodded. "As good as any."

Raina's head whipped from one man to the other. Talk about being treated like chopped liver. Why were they ignoring her? Weren't they supposed to duke it out for her favor? "Ahem."

Sonny raised an eyebrow at Matthew as if to say "she's yours."

Raina ground her teeth. This was beyond annoying. She was supposed to be the link between these two men. Now here they were making their own little deal without her.

"Rainy, I know you find this hard to believe, but not everything is about you," Matthew said. One corner of his lip curled like he was trying to hide his amusement.

Sonny, on the other hand, had a full-blown smirk on his face. "We wouldn't want you swooning when Matthew and I mark off our steps."

Raina ignored their amusement and addressed Sonny instead. "I want to continue our earlier conversation. We need to talk to the Lows."

"Just leave it to the police," Matthew said. "If they had anything to do with the explosion, you don't want to get involved with them."

"But—"

Sonny cut his eyes at Matthew but kept silent.

Raina knew Sonny wouldn't ask for her help in front of Matthew nor would he speak as openly as he did when the two of them were alone. In other words, Matthew was cramping her style.

"Po Po needs your help," Matthew said. "She has commandeered the library as her command center." He glanced at Sonny. "The police have released Jerry's body for burial."

16

LAST RITES

Raina was still miffed by the time she got to the library. Matthew was probably doing his cave man thing with Sonny. She was lucky he didn't pee on her to mark his territory. She snorted at the image. Or maybe not. He wasn't the type to get territorial when it came to her affections. Her safety, on the other hand, was a different story.

But what if he did a little digging into the Nine Dragons? It was rare for someone on his side of the tracks to have access to the headquarters of a criminal organization. And Matthew still had connections with the feds. She didn't want to be involved in trying to take down a criminal organization. That's for Matthew and his friends.

Her grandma had covered the massive formal desk with papers. Somehow, she'd gotten hold of a laptop. Even more amazing was the sight of Po Po and Cat making separate calls to the same list from the sofa. Must be the people they needed to notify for the funeral tomorrow. With her grandma at the helm, it looked like Jerry would be buried within three days as tradition dictated.

For the next three hours, Raina helped with the calls. Her grandma managed to find an online Buddhist monk to perform the funeral service. This wouldn't sit well with the local temple once they found out this online business was undercutting them in price and convenience. She even arranged the traditional follow-up prayer ceremonies and the forty-ninth-day posthumous ritual.

"We don't need the official mourners, do we?" Po Po asked, glancing up. "That would be extra."

Raina shrugged. "Yes, we do. There wouldn't be enough keening without them. Who's driving to Chinatown to pick up the mourning costumes and the other ceremonial gear like joss paper?"

"I can send someone," Cat said. "Just give me a list of what you need."

As her grandma proceeded to write down the items for the funeral, Raina wondered how she should broach the subject of the murder investigation.

"What are you going to do after all this is done?" Raina asked Cat.

The Nine Dragons Enforcer frowned at her. "What do you mean?"

Raina ticked the points off her fingers. "Jerry is dead. Lily will probably escape from the hospital so she won't have to come back to this place. Kwan Gong is poised to have another heart attack again. He probably would have to slow down. What is to stop you from walking away from this life?"

Cat gaped at her. Apparently, this thought hadn't

crossed her mind. "I can't go. I have enemies. I need the Nine Dragons protection."

"Not if you disappeared. The United States is a big place. And with so many Hispanic people, you could blend right in."

"People like me can't have normal lives. I'll probably die young. I just hope I don't see it coming."

Raina felt bad for the other woman. "You're not a slave. You're in control of your own destiny. There's always hope for a better future."

Cat sneered at her naïveté. "For rich girls like you, yes, life will always get better. But for people like me, I would end up dead in a dumpster someday and nobody would even feel a twinge of sadness."

"My family is rich, but I'm not. I would feel sadness. I would never want that to happen to you. With the organization in chaos, this is the perfect time for you to disappear."

Cat shook her head, her eyes darkening with emotion. "You're as good as rich. You'll always have options I don't have. You can't go very far on a few hundred bucks."

Po Po handed Cat the list. "If money is the only thing keeping you here, then I can help."

ON THE DAY of the funeral, it was bright and warm by nine o'clock in the morning. It was a day made for the beach rather than funeral white. The family had to use a funeral parlor so it wouldn't bring bad luck to the surviving elder in the family home.

Unfortunately, this meant several armed triad members surrounded the premises. The funeral director developed a nervous throat-clearing tick when the setup party rolled in. Apparently, her grandma hadn't warned him about Jerry's celebrity status when she made the arrangements and rented the entire funeral home for the next twenty-four hours.

In the viewing room, a poster-size portrait of Jerry hung on the front wall. The closed casket took center stage with white wreaths displayed next to its foot. They opted for a closed casket given the swelling in Jerry's face. Joss sticks burned in an urn on the low table in front of the casket. The heady fragrance would become a bleary haze by this evening and unbearable by the morning.

In his loose white funeral robe, Kwan Gong knelt to the left of the casket, burning joss paper and funeral money in the metal bowl in front of him. The official mourners ringed him, wailing loud enough to be heard, but not loud enough to drown out every sound. It was also modulated so you could ignore them as one would a ceiling fan. Boy, they were good and well worth the extra cost.

As predicted, Lily had hightailed it from the hospital in the middle of the night. With no wife to honor the dead, Kwan Gong had abandoned the tradition which prevented an elder from mourning his child in public. At least he didn't put on the sackcloth hood meant for the deceased's wife and children.

Sonny stood at the entrance next to the funeral gong to greet the guests. Matthew had wisely opted to stay in a hotel room in town. He was only a phone call away if she needed him. It wouldn't do to have a cop among the robbers at a highly emotional event like this funeral.

As the mourners paid their respects by the casket, Raina studied them from her post next to the white wreaths. She handed the lit joss sticks to anyone wishing to pay their respects. Her grandma would relieve her after her errand with Cat to pick up "forgotten" supplies from the mansion. Somehow, Raina doubted she would see the Hispanic woman again.

Detective Bibb showed up an hour after the monk started chanting the Buddhist scriptures by the funeral gong. He stood in the entryway, clearly out of his depth. Maybe he thought the funeral service would have wrapped up by the time he arrived.

The chanting would go on for the next twenty-four hours. Another monk waited in one of the smaller viewing rooms to relieve his partner. When the detective glanced in Raina's direction, she made a small bowing motion and pointed at the front. It was too late for him to back away now.

As the detective approached the casket, the entire room focused on him. A couple triad members rested their hands on poorly hidden gun holsters. Sonny's face became even more expressionless. One flick of his finger and Detective Bibb would become a human pincushion.

Kwan Gong paid no attention to the rising tension in the room, dropping joss paper, funeral money, and tears into the flames in the metal bowl. Raina hoped he wouldn't end up with a cloud of bad luck in his remaining years for loving his child.

Detective Bibb stopped a couple feet away from the

casket. He hesitated. The deep crow's feet around his eyes tightened even more.

Raina handed him a joss stick and pointed at the urn. If someone pulled out a gun, she would jump behind the casket. Her head throbbed from the thick fragrant smoke and rising testosterone in the room. *Come on, just pretend to pay your respect...*

The detective bowed to the casket and placed the joss stick in the urn. He mumbled something to Kwan Gong and stepped aside to take a seat in an empty row.

Sonny ignored the detective, and the mourners started to drift into groups, depending on where their loyalties lay. Even though Jerry could no longer be Dai Lo —being dead and all—the leadership position could pass on to someone else within the criminal organization.

Kwan Gong had shown the soft underside of his belly with his mourning, and now the Piranhas were circling and waiting for a nibble. Jerry's death made Sonny's precarious position as Dai Lo even worse.

If he could rally the Nine Dragons against a common enemy then maybe he stood a chance. But who could this enemy be? The Italian mob? Would helping the Black Tigers help or worsen his position? Regardless, he had to make a decision. Freddie Low was cashing in his favor, and the honor of the Nine Dragons would be questioned if Sonny did nothing.

Raina's head throbbed even more. She didn't want to be involved in the Nine Dragons politics. With Detective Bibb in the room, nothing would happen beyond scheming and the making of alliances. The coup, if there would be one, wouldn't happen until tomorrow after

Jerry's burial. Hopefully, Raina could get her answers from Sonny before then.

Po Po came into the room, glanced around and headed straight for Kwan Gong. For some crazy reason, her grandma seemed immune to the undercurrent in the room. Maybe her grandma had it right. Once you were established as a wacky old lady, everyone ignored or dismissed you.

Raina gestured at a henchman staring out the window to take her post. She needed some air. The tightness in her shoulder blades didn't help with her headache.

She strode out of the main viewing room and walked past the smaller one, which the pallbearers had taken over as a gambling hall. Since the pallbearers had an all-night vigil to watch for Jerry's spirit, gambling was allowed to help them stay awake. Some customs were just unexplainable to an outsider.

Raina hunched her shoulders and trotted down the street. She wanted to break out into a jog, but it would be too unseemly being this close to the funeral parlor. She didn't know where she was going, but she needed to clear her mind.

Since the explosion, she had been reacting to events rather than staying one step ahead of things. She couldn't help but feel as if someone was keeping her busy so she wouldn't have time to think about the murder investigation.

Footsteps pounded nearby, keeping pace with her. She glanced over to find Detective Bibb next to her. Great. She wasn't in the mood for accusations or innuendo about her guilt. If he started that up again, he was gonna get it.

She glanced behind her. A henchman followed them from a distance, giving them a semblance of privacy. She sighed. How did she end up being the Grand Marshall to a parade she didn't want to be in?

Sonny probably wanted to make sure she had a bodyguard in case the other faction or one of his enemies tried something. She understood his intentions, but it reminded her of how suffocating this kind of life could be. No wonder Lily wanted out.

"Why are you following me?" Raina whispered to the detective.

"I want to thank you for your help back there, Miss Sun," Detective Bibb replied. Her earlier assessment that he liked to spend time outdoors was correct. He took wide strides to keep up with her trots. No huffing and puffing on his part. Geez, the man was in good shape despite the small paunch around his middle.

"Think nothing of it." When they approached a coffee shop, she said, "This is my stop." She went in, and Detective Bibb came in after her.

She spun around. "Just spill it. What do you want? If you are planning to threaten me, save your breath. I had nothing to do with Jerry's death, and you can't pin anything on me."

The henchman lounged outside the shop, leaning against a parking meter and smoking. He didn't seem concerned with the detective following Raina into the shop. Maybe he got directions not to interfere unless it was a life or death situation.

"Let me buy you a drink," the detective said.

Raina snorted. Seriously? Well, she could save five bucks by taking his offer.

After they got their drinks, they found a table at the far end of the room.

Raina sipped her iced caramel macchiato. She had no idea why the detective would seek her out, given his earlier animosity, but it wasn't to give her a gold star.

Detective Bibb cleared his throat, glancing at the henchman outside the shop window. "Have you seen Cat Hernandez? She murdered Jerry Kwan."

17

A BIGGER MOUSETRAP

Raina choked on her coffee, spraying droplets across the small table in front of them. What the heck? Did her grandma just help a criminal escape? Even if Raina were a poor judge of character, her grandma wouldn't have been. No, the detective had it wrong.

Detective Bibb jerked back but calmly wiped his face with a napkin. "So I take it that you know where Miss Hernandez is."

"Actually, I have no idea. Why do you suspect Cat is the killer?"

"She has every reason to hate the Kwans. She was a runaway when Kwan Gong found her ten years ago and lured her into a prostitution ring."

"But Jerry Kwan rescued her from that life. Why would she turn around and kill him?" Raina asked. She replayed the conversations she had with Cat. The Nine Dragons Enforcer was still a victim to the criminal organization, not the predator the detective thought she was.

Raina shook her head. "She's not the killer. It's one of the Lows...or both."

He raised an eyebrow. When he replied his voice was heavy with doubt. "Is that right? What reason would they have for killing Jerry?"

Raina hesitated. Her gut was telling her it had something to do with Jerry and Lily's past. For some couples, it was hard to let go of the first love. Look at her and Matthew. In the last decade, they had reconnected several times. It always ended in blood and tears, and yet, neither one of them could let their past go.

She glanced at the sparkling diamond ring on her hand. And here she was, once again, wearing the same ring from Matthew. Sure, it had new window dressing on it this time—rubies from his grandma—but it was still essentially the same ring. This probably meant she was engaged to Matthew again, but it didn't bother her for some reason. What changed?

"You were saying?" the detective said, interrupting her thoughts.

"You haven't touched your coffee. I don't trust anyone who would waste good coffee," Raina said, stalling to gather her thoughts. She had a feeling they would sound cuckoo to an outsider.

Detective Bibb raised an eyebrow and took a sip of his coffee. "Happy now?"

Raina grinned. He sounded just like Matthew. "Are you a romantic man? Do you believe in fate?"

The detective blinked. Raina could sense him closing in as if afraid she might ask personal questions he didn't have answers to. The silence stretched for a heartbeat.

For a second, she wondered if he was a workaholic without a life outside of the office.

"What does my love life have to do with the case?" he finally asked.

"Fate plays a big role in the Chinese culture. Sometimes our actions are dictated by this belief that you can't run away from fate."

"Oookay," he said slowly. His face asked where she was going with this conversation.

"What if Jerry and Myling believed they were fated to be together, even though both of them were married to someone else? They were lovers in their teens," Raina said.

Detective Bibb sipped his coffee. "Are you suggesting the two of them had an affair?"

"Not necessarily a physical one. An emotional one could be just as devastating in a marriage," Raina said, thinking about her grandfather and his secret family.

"I still don't get it. Do we have a jealous husband who killed his romantic rival?"

"Maybe. Or we could have a wife who wants out from fate."

"I'm confused. Are you talking about Lily Kwan?"

"Lily wants out, but I don't think she killed Jerry."

"So Myling did. What evidence do you have?"

"None."

"But Myling was engaged to Sonny at one point?"

Raina shrugged. "She probably thought it would keep her close to Jerry. Second best is better than nothing. And Sonny is a man."

"What's that supposed to mean?" The detective's tone sounded offended.

"Wouldn't you be flattered if an attractive woman threw herself at you? Unlike other women, Myling is vetted. She is accepted by the inner circle of the Kwan family and the Nine Dragons. It's easy for Sonny to let his guard down with her."

"Armchair psychiatry isn't going to convict a murderer. How can you be so sure of this?"

"Because of fate. If you let it run out of control, you can hate as deeply as you love each other," Raina said.

She told him about the satisfied smirk on Myling's face when she told her ex-lover she was pregnant in the foyer on the night of the birthday party. Raina hadn't known the significance at the time, but it all made sense now that she knew Jerry and Myling had been lovers. Heck, she might be the mistress Lily spoke of.

Raina took a deep breath. This would probably get her thrown in jail, but the truth had to come out at some point, and this was as good as any. Now that the Kwan family owed her grandma for arranging the funeral, Raina felt she was in a better position to ignore what Sonny wanted.

"There's more," she said. "Jerry texted someone before his death. To have a secret meeting." She told the detective the truth about Jerry falling on her lap and the cellphone in her purse.

By the time she was done, Detective Bibb's expression became even sterner. "I know I tampered with the crime scene, but I was afraid to go against Sonny. Even now, I don't know how he would react if he found out I told you the truth."

"Then why are you telling me this now?"

"Because you wouldn't find out about this otherwise.

But please be careful with this information. Sonny's position as Dai Lo is precarious. I don't want him to get hurt by this."

"So you support what he does for a living?"

"No, but I don't want to be the reason he gets hurt. Once I'm out of the picture, it's not on my conscience."

"Fair enough, Miss Sun."

They sipped their coffee for several minutes. The normal coffee shop noise filled the space between them.

Raina thought about Matthew and how much she wanted to hold him at the moment. It didn't matter how long or hard she ran. Fate had a way of mocking their efforts. A decade of running for both of them hadn't gotten them very far from each other. And the last thing she wanted was to turn their love into hate.

Finally Detective Bibb broke the silence. "We need to build a mousetrap."

RAINA BLINKED, her thoughts caught up in her own problems. "What?"

The bell above the door jingled, and she glanced over to see her grandma making a beeline for them. The lounging henchman flicked a glance into the shop and tapped out another cigarette from his pack.

Po Po pulled up a chair between Raina and Detective Bibb. "What's up, peeps? Are we forming a plan to nab the bad guy?"

"How did you find us?" Detective Bibb asked.

Her grandma hooked a thumb at the henchmen. "I just had to look for a Chinese youth with a shaggy goatee, sagging pants, and exposed boxers. Easy peasy." She tapped the bracelet on Raina's hand.

Raina had forgotten about the GPS tracker in the bracelet. "Shouldn't you be at the funeral parlor handing out joss sticks?"

Po Po waved dismissively. "That's low-level work. It's for people like Mr. Shaggy out there. I'm meant for the big time. So what's the plan?"

Raina gave Detective Bibb a significant look. He'd better not try to involve her grandma in this mousetrap scheme of his.

He ignored her. "I'm trying to convince your grand-daughter to help me set a trap for Jerry Kwan's killer."

Po Po's eyes lit up. "Of course we will do anything we can to help bring the killer to justice. So who is the killer?"

Detective Bibb repeated Raina's theory. He even added a line about how he always suspected Raina found Jerry's body. Yep, he certainly sounded like he'd pieced everything together well before today.

Po Po wiggled her eyebrows at Raina. "Well, now aren't you the smart one. So what's the plan?"

Both Detective Bibb and Po Po looked at Raina expectantly.

Raina sipped her coffee. She could understand her grandma, but for the detective to look at her as the master schemer, now this didn't happen every day. He was probably trying to test her. "I don't know. We could always try to get Myling to confess to the crime."

"Fat chance of that," Po Po said. "She is sly. The only way to get her to confess would be to provoke her."

Raina groaned. "I don't want to poke the bear."

"We can always tell Sonny what we suspected," Po Po said. "He'll take care of it."

"No!" Raina said.

"No," Detective Bibb said.

They looked at each other.

Raina didn't want to be responsible for Sonny throwing Myling into a lake. At least she was on the same page with the detective regarding vigilante justice.

Her grandma shrugged. "It was just a suggestion. There's no need to get your panties in a knot."

"It would be hard to get Myling alone to get a confession," Detective Bibb said. "She must have her own security team. And once the Lows return to New York City, she'll be practically untouchable."

Raina stood. "We need to get back to the funeral. Let's table this until the detective comes up with a plan." She couldn't risk her grandma getting involved in taking down Jerry's killer.

Detective Bibb held the door open for them. "Thank you for your time, ladies. Let's count on getting in touch tomorrow. In the meantime, I'll check to see if Matthew Louie wants to have lunch." He nodded at them and crossed the street.

Raina and Po Po strolled back to the funeral parlor together. The henchman trailed them by half a block.

"How did the errand with Cat go?" Raina asked.

"Fine. She'll probably have to take a plane ride to get this special joss paper for the funeral," Po Po said.

"Seriously?"

"I don't know, Rainy. I gave her some money and told her to have a good life."

Raina slung an arm around her grandma's shoulders. "Po Po, you're a soft, squishy marshmallow."

"Hey, don't go around telling people that. It'll ruin my biker chick reputation."

Raina didn't have the heart to tell her grandma that an eighties biker chick wasn't a good look for her. She was already sweating enough in this heat under all the leather.

"Detective Bibb initially thought Cat was the killer," she said.

Po Po snorted. "Did he tell you why?"

"Actually I think he was trying to bait me into telling him what I know."

"It worked, right?"

"Sure, we'll go with that."

Her grandma patted Raina's cheek. "Smart girl."

By the time they got to the funeral parlor, Raina needed to use the restroom to freshen up. Her grandma opted to return to the main viewing room. According to her grandma, sweat would keep the punks away from her.

The restroom was tucked at the back of the building in a hallway with frosted glass windows. When Raina pushed open the heavy wood door, she caught a glimpse of Myling before she went into a stall. She heard vomiting noises. Yikes! Must be the morning sickness.

Raina backed out of the restroom and closed the door softly. She pulled out her cell phone and texted her grandma.

"The bird has landed. In the restroom. Come record conversation."

She turned on the voice recorder app on her phone

and tucked her cell phone back into her purse, leaving the zipper open. It was the best she could do. The only other place she could put her cell phone was in her bra and a lump this size would be questioned.

When Raina heard the click of the lock in the stall, she pushed open the door again. "Hi, Myling. I didn't expect to see you here." She stepped into the restroom, blocking the exit. "Oh, right, you and Jerry were lovers once. Of course you would be at his funeral."

18

THE WRONG BAIT

Myling glanced at Raina's reflection in the mirror, wiping her mouth with a wet paper towel.

Raina felt a twinge of guilt for bothering her at a time like this, but this could be the only chance she got to get a confession out of Myling. Once she was firmly by her husband's side, who would dare bother her then? Not unless the person was insane. Heck, Raina might be insane now.

"There's no need to be catty. I don't care you're with Sonny," Myling said.

Raina blinked. That was right. Myling wasn't there when Sonny and his grandfather had their blow-up fight. Now how could Raina use this to her advantage? She pretended to smirk. "But you would care if I were with Jerry. Is that why you killed him—you can't stand he's with Lily now?"

Myling's eyes narrowed, studying Raina. She threw the paper towel into the trash. "Your accusation will piss off my husband. You don't want Freddie Low for an enemy."

Raina ignored her threats. "So he knows you were with Jerry first, then Sonny, and he was the last choice?"

She couldn't believe the fighting words leaving her mouth. There were several dozen people within screaming distance. It wasn't like Myling could attack her without making a ruckus.

Myling stiffened with anger. "How dare you? Like you don't have a past?" She stalked over. "Are you going to move or do you plan to knock over a pregnant woman?"

Raina sidestepped. Okay, so she was a wimp when it came to confrontation.

Myling marched past, swinging her purse over her shoulder. The bag hit Raina on the chest, but the other woman didn't seem to notice or care.

Po Po came in half a minute later. "What happened? I saw Myling leaving."

Raina rubbed her chest. "I wasn't going to knock over a pregnant woman."

"But she could be the killer."

"I'm starting to second guess myself. It's been over a decade since Jerry and Myling were lovers."

"That's not true. Remember the text messages. They seemed pretty recent to me. And Myling visits the Kwan residence regularly, using Kwan Gong as an excuse. Trust your instincts, Rainy, there's something here. If she's not the killer, then it's her husband."

"Okay, should we go poke that bear?"

"I thought you would never ask."

They left the restroom and headed toward the main viewing room, keeping an eye out for Freddie Low. As long as they didn't leave the premises, Raina felt relatively safe in engaging the Lows. With Nine Dragons members crawling on top of each other, the Lows couldn't touch her. And if they ended up having nothing to do with the murder, she would apologize later.

A quick peek inside the main viewing room showed Myling speaking furiously to Sonny. Raina quickly ducked back outside before they saw her. If they were talking about her, she didn't want to know about it. They found Freddie out back in the rear parking lot, making a phone call. They waited inside the building for him to finish his conversation.

"This time, follow my lead," Po Po whispered.

"I think you should let me do it," Raina whispered back.

"You had your chance with Myling. My turn now."

Before Raina could say anything else, Freddie ended his phone call and spotted the two of them loitering in the doorway. He nodded at them and waited for them to move out of his way.

"Mr. Low, I forgot to congratulate you. We just found out Myling is expecting," Po Po said, standing in the middle of the doorway.

The only way Freddie could get back into the building would be to knock over a little granny. Smooth move.

"Thank you, Po Po," Freddie said. "We have been trying for a while."

"Are you sure the baby is yours though?" Po Po asked, and she wiggled her eyebrows suggestively. "I've heard Jerry and Myling were mighty friendly together."

Freddie reared back like her grandma had socked

him. Maybe she did. His face turned ashen. "Who told you this lie? I will kill him."

Raina shivered at the menace in his voice. She grabbed her grandma's arm and dragged her back. "That's what everyone in the Nine Dragons is saying. It's common knowledge they were lovers until the two of you got married."

Freddie pulled out a gun, turned around, and slammed the gun against a garbage can lid repeatedly. He screamed a few words she couldn't repeat.

Raina jumped in front of Po Po and walked them backward into the building, keeping her eyes on Freddie the entire time. She pulled the hair stick out of her purse, holding it in front of her like a knife.

When the lid was nothing more than a deformed shape, he put the gun back into his holster. He straightened his gray suit and took a deep breath.

Raina and her grandma were inside the building by this time, but still within sight distance. A bead of sweat ran down the small of her back.

"Sorry," Freddie called out. "I have anger management issues. I'm working on it."

Raina acknowledged him with a nod but continued to walk backward until he was out of sight. She dragged her grandma back into the main viewing room.

They collapsed into the back row of chairs. Raina's trembling legs couldn't have supported her any further. Her heart pounded against her chest.

She was so stupid. What was she thinking? Did she think she could get a confession when the police couldn't touch the Lows? All she had on her was a hair stick and pepper spray.

～

"ARE YOU OKAY?" Po Po asked, breaking into Raina's thoughts.

Raina glanced over at Po Po. Her grandma seemed perfectly at ease. "I'm still trying to keep from pooping my pants. How come you're so calm?"

"If you'd lived as long as I have, uh"—Po Po gave Raina a sideways glance—"fifty-five years, you've pretty much seen everything."

Raina ignored her grandma's comment on her age. She lost or gained years as it suited her. Apparently today she was the same age as Raina's mother. "You're right. We're safe enough in this crowd. We'll get Sonny to talk this evening, and by tomorrow we'll be on our way home."

Po Po patted Raina's knees. "Eyes on the prize, girl. We'll do what we can to help the police, but we're here to find the truth about my husband's"—her grandma's voice cracked, and she cleared her throat—"other family."

Raina hugged her grandma. "That's right."

"I'm hungry. Where's that funeral director? He was supposed to have a room set aside for the spread," Po Po said, getting up. "I'm going to look for the food." Her grandma left the room.

Raina probably should go back to her post and hand out joss sticks, but as her grandma said, that was low-level work. Her talents lay elsewhere. Although, poking the bear didn't seem to be one of them.

Freddie came into the viewing room and made a beeline toward Myling, who was sitting with her face in her hands in a chair right next to the official mourners.

That Raina hadn't noticed Myling until now was unsettling. She must be more rattled by Freddie's "anger management issue" than she let on to her grandma.

Freddie said something to his wife, and she shook her head. He grabbed his wife's arm and hauled her up.

Sonny glanced over at the couple, but he didn't interfere. However, several Nine Dragons members frowned at Freddie. At least no one fingered their guns.

Myling had grown up as a de facto princess in the organization, and even though she was married, it didn't mean she was without her supporters. Too bad she couldn't bring an alliance to a marriage, or she could have married Jerry.

The Lows left without a shoot-out, and everything resumed. The professional mourners kept mourning, and the Buddhist monk kept chanting. People came and went. Most of them wouldn't stay for the vigil.

Raina's cell phone dinged, and she checked her text message. She wouldn't be able to add marketing to her resume after all. The Chinese Opera Company fired her for missing too many days of work. At least she didn't have to return to the dreary office.

Fifteen minutes later, Po Po returned to the main viewing room. "The catering truck is on its way. It will be another ten minutes. Someone called in sick and they're scrambling."

Raina's stomach growled. Why didn't she grab a pastry with the coffee earlier? "That's good to know."

She glanced at the display on her cell phone. It was already one o'clock. A few more hours and she could return to the mansion with the Kwan family, leaving the pallbearers to watch for Jerry's spirit.

"What happened with the Lows?" Po Po asked. "They passed me on the way out when I was still on the phone with the caterers."

"Not much. He grabbed her and got some dirty looks."

"I think that's the last we'll see of them. If they were smart, they would hightail it back to New York City."

"What about their Italian mob problem?"

"They'll have to figure something out," Sonny said from behind them. "The Nine Dragons are not getting involved."

Raina glanced back. How much of their conversation had he overheard? And if the Lows were heading back to New York City, how would they be brought to justice for Jerry's death? One or both of them were responsible. She still believed it was Myling, but she had no proof other than what her gut told her.

If she told Sonny what she suspected, he could prevent them from leaving town. But she was afraid of his methods, and she didn't want to start a war between the two triads. There was always collateral damage when rival gangs shoot 'em up. Maybe she should call Detective Bibb to fill him in.

"The gears are turning in your head. Should I be worried?" Sonny said.

"But I thought you owed them a favor," Raina said.

Sunny shrugged. "If it's within my personal power I'll grant it, but war with a rival organization isn't something I would take on without the Elders' support."

"I need to make a phone call," Raina said, getting up. She stepped outside into the hallway and out back so she could have some privacy. She didn't want any of the Nine

Dragons members to eavesdrop on her conversation with the police.

The catering van pulled into the back parking lot. The Nine Dragons member posted at the driveway must have waved it through. Raina scrolled through the recent call list on her phone for Detective Bibb's number.

She could sense someone approaching and she automatically sidestepped so the person could get into the building without having to maneuver around her with a tray of food. A sharp pain flared from the base of her neck until it engulfed her entire body. Then it was lights out.

19

TAKING A DRIVE

When Raina became aware of her surroundings again, she was in a fetal position. Her body swayed to a lulling motion, making it easy to keep her eyes closed and drift off again. She fought for consciousness. If she fell asleep now, she might never wake again.

She opened her eyes, but couldn't see anything. Coarse fabric brushed against her face. Duct tape bound her hands behind her back. Tape also covered her mouth. Her heart pounded with fear and her breaths came out in sharp puffs. An image of a coffin rose in her mind.

Raina's first instinct was to scream, but she suppressed it and forced herself to take deep calming breaths, drawing in whiffs of stale onions and earth. She wasn't dead yet, and if she panicked she wouldn't have a chance. She stuffed the fear into the far corner of her mind and focused on how to get out of her situation.

As long as her captor believed Raina was unconscious, she still had an advantage. The swaying motion stopped suddenly, and she skidded until she hit something hard. It knocked the wind out of her, but she bit her lower lip to stay quiet. A tear rolled down her cheek, and she blinked rapidly to clear her vision. This wasn't the time to break down.

The fabric shifted, and a gap appeared. She was lying on the floor of a vehicle, and judging by the smell and size, probably the catering van. But why would the driver kidnap her? Did he work for the Lows? Through the gap, she could see the back of the driver's head.

"Idiot!" muttered someone. The driver glanced back. Myling!

Raina's eyes slammed shut. Two Mississippi's later, she opened them to see Myling had returned her attention to the road. Raina strained her ears but couldn't tell if Freddie was with her.

Her fingers patted the area behind her, looking for something to cut the duct tape. Something pricked her hands, and she instinctively jerked back from the sharp object. She cautiously reached for the object, touching its length. A steak knife. Hallelujah! It must have shifted over when Myling slammed on the brakes.

Raina sawed at the duct tape. When she nicked her arm by accident, she jumped again. She glanced up, but Myling was busy with one eye on the road and the other on her cell phone. Was she texting? It would be ironic if they got into a car accident. But with Raina's luck and without a seatbelt, she would probably end up thrown through a window and onto the side of the road.

Myling pulled off the road. She slowed down, but the car bounced even more like they were on an uneven dirt path. Branches scraped against the windows. Yep, they were off-road somewhere. Myling's cell phone rang, but she ignored it.

Raina knew once Myling stopped the van, she would have one chance to make an escape. Sweat drenched her back. The musty blanket or sack Myling had thrown over her didn't help. Her moist hands made it difficult to grip the steak knife properly. She nicked herself again but kept sawing at the duct tape. She would probably die from blood loss before she got the darn thing off.

The knife clinked against something, and Raina held her breath. Myling didn't even glance over. The van thumped along the road, making enough noise to drown out everything else.

The knife tapped the metal again. Of course! Her grandma's bracelet with the GPS tracker. Raina just had to stay alive long enough for her grandma to locate her. Easy peasy.

One last tug with the steak knife and her hands were free. She didn't dare to remove the duct tape from her mouth. There was no way she could stop herself from screaming. She tucked the knife into her waistband behind her back. Keeping an eye on Myling, Raina patted the area around her, looking for another weapon. Her hands encountered leather, and she pulled it closer for a look. It was her purse.

She unzipped it and pulled out her cell phone. She tapped the recorder app and tucked the phone into her back pocket. Even if it didn't record a confession, it would provide some information about her last moments if need be. Everything in her phone was backed up to the cloud, and her grandma had her password.

Myling's cell phone rang again. She glanced at the caller ID, dismissed the call, and tossed the phone behind her.

It slammed into Raina's forehead, and she winced in pain. She bit her lip again to keep from crying out. The cell phone rang again. The display said the caller was Freddie. Myling ignored the ringing phone, and the van kept bouncing along the road.

Raina dug into her purse and pulled out the pepper spray and hair stick. She tucked the pepper spray into her bra and stuck the hair stick into her ponytail. She took another calming breath. Should she stall by talking to Myling or go into ninja attack mode when the van stopped?

The van hit a bump and dipped, making a loud squeal and crunch that bode well. It inched forward for another foot or so and stopped. Myling cursed in Chinese, slamming her palms on the steering wheel. She jerked open the driver door and went outside. The cursing continued outside about the mud. Like this would help with their current predicament.

The van door opened, and a fresh breeze drifted inside, lifting a curl away from Raina's face. With her eyes closed, Raina took a deep breath. Freedom. She could—

Myling jerked the blanket off and slapped Raina's face. "Wake up, sleepyhead. I need you to walk."

Raina's face stung, and she squinted at the brilliant sunlight streaming in from behind Myling's shoulders. They were in a forest area. Probably close to a lake or bog judging by the mud covering her captor's pants legs.

"What happened?" Raina asked. What came out was

a muffled, garbled sound from behind the duct tape. And Sonny said she couldn't act.

Myling pulled a gun out from her pocket, pointing it at Raina. "I need you to move, or I'll shoot your shoulder. The next time I ask again, I'll shoot your other shoulder. We'll keep going until either you're moving or dead."

Raina shivered. The fear she'd locked up earlier slammed into her. Her chest heaved, and she couldn't get enough air. The bright light around Myling became whiter. Her eyes rolled, unable to focus. Oh, geez...

Myling slammed the butt of the gun on Raina's leg.

A sharp flash of pain jolted Raina out of her panic. Her teary eyes focused on a lump next to her. She blinked. Was that a person? Was this the driver of the catering van? She had bumped into him when Myling slammed on the brakes earlier. Raina couldn't see any visible injuries on him, but his ashen pallor and stillness spoke volumes.

"Are you coming, or do we need more incentive?" Myling asked.

Raina shivered at the chill in her captor's voice. She kept her hands behind her back and shuffled forward with her legs, inching along like an earthworm.

"Will you hurry up?" Myling said. "If you hadn't mentioned my affair with Jerry to Freddie, he wouldn't have gone on this stupid rampage about needing a DNA test." She jabbed a finger at her stomach. "How am I supposed to fake this?"

"So that's why you had to kill Jerry," Raina said. It came out in a garbled groan.

Myling ripped the duct tape and several layers of skin off of Raina's mouth.

"Eowww!" Raina screamed. "You crazy bi—"

Myling pointed the gun at Raina's forehead, and Raina shut up. "I'm not crazy. I needed to get Jerry out of my life."

"Good luck with that, seeing as now you're having his baby," Raina said, shoving her legs forward. Her kick slammed into Myling's chest.

Myling stumbled backward, slipping on the mud. She fired the gun, but the shot went wild.

Raina jumped out of the van. The momentum carried her forward until she straddled Myling on the muddy ground. She grabbed Myling's hand, slamming it on the ground. The gun plopped onto the mud somewhere. She jabbed Myling in the collar with the hair stick, but the stick snapped in half in Raina's hands.

Myling screamed and bucked, knocking Raina off her perch. Raina landed on the side of her face. Cold mud oozed into her mouth. Yuck! Myling jerked at Raina's waistband. The steak knife!

Raina rolled onto her back, pinched the knife and Myling's hand onto the ground. She pulled the pepper spray out of her bra, blasting Myling in the face. Or at least she hoped it was Myling's face. The mud dripping down Raina's cheek distorted much of her view.

In the distance, tires crunched and someone shouted. A siren wailed.

Unfortunately, the wind shifted and some of the pepper spray came back on Raina. Her eyes and sinuses exploded in pain, and she burst into a coughing fit. She crawled on hands and knees toward the noise, trying to put some distance between her and Myling.

There was more shouting, and footsteps approached

them, crunching leaves and branches. And that was how Matthew found Raina—choking on her own pepper spray with a bruise the size of Texas on her forehead from Myling's cell phone. She sure knew how to make a man hot and heavy.

20

NO MORE SECRETS

The next morning, the knocking on the door woke Raina. She had returned to Matthew's hotel room after the paramedics checked her out and police released her late in the evening. Po Po had returned to the Kwan mansion but said she would be by in the morning.

Raina glanced at the time on her cell phone. Eight o'clock. Couldn't her grandma let her sleep in? The note on the nightstand said Matthew was having breakfast with Detective Bibb, and he would bring her back something yummy. She hoped he meant food.

She stumbled out of bed and opened the door. "I hope you have coffee with you."

Sonny jiggled the ice in the plastic cup he held in front of him. "Your wish is my command."

Raina blinked. Was she dressed? She glanced down at herself. She had on Matthew's *Gold Springs Police* T-shirt, leaving large swaths of her exposed. She held up a finger. "Give me a minute." She closed the door, leaning against it to take a deep breath. No more rest for the weary. And boy, was she weary.

It took more like ten minutes to do her morning business and throw on her clothes. Matthew had them laundered the night before while she slept. She could get used to a Chinese man who did laundry.

Raina texted Matthew to let him know Sonny was here. She didn't want to surprise Matthew if he walked in on them. She opened the door and gestured for Sonny to come in.

Sonny glanced around the hotel room, probably to assess for danger. There wasn't much to see—a bed, two nightstands, and a TV. "Well, I'm glad you made your choice. I'm sick of watching the two of you make puppy eyes at each other."

He was dressed from head to toe in black with a white armband to show his family was in mourning. The last time she'd seen him this relaxed was when he proposed their bargain.

"I don't need to make puppy eyes at a man."

"If you say so," he said. His tone said otherwise. "Do you want to go out for breakfast?"

Raina shook her head and went to sit on the bed. "We need to talk, and I don't want anyone to interrupt us."

Sonny closed the door and followed her in. He shifted from foot to foot until she reached for the iced caramel macchiato he held out to her. "Thank you for all that you've done for my family. You're the only one who cared enough to help me."

Raina sipped her coffee, letting the silence drag out. She didn't bother correcting him. It was blind luck more than intention that had recorded Myling's confession. "How did Kwan Gong take the news?"

"He thinks it's karma coming to bite us. He's talking about becoming a monk to atone for everything he did. He wants me to leave the family business."

"You mean leave the Nine Dragons?"

Sonny grimaced, stretching the scar on the side of his face. "It's not that easy to leave this life. Not at my level."

Raina nodded. Too many enemies and too many ties. "How did Myling get the catering van?"

"According to the driver, he was at a stoplight when a woman came up to him, waving a gun. She got in and told him to drive to the funeral parlor. Then she knocked you out, got him to drag you in the van, and then she gave him the same treatment."

"Will the driver be okay?"

Sonny nodded. "Myling is claiming temporary insanity from the pregnancy hormones."

"Seriously?"

Sonny shrugged. "What do I know? I've never been pregnant."

Raina snorted. Not her problem anymore. "Why did my grandfather marry another woman in China and keep that family hidden for the last fifty years? You said he searched for her?"

Her grandfather had traveled from Hong Kong to China under the guise of working on the Great Leap Forward policies in 1962.

"She was his half-sister and pregnant at the time. A rape victim."

"I don't understand. He married his sister?"

"His secret sister. She was adopted by a family in a remote village. No one knew about the connection."

"Why didn't he move his sister to Hong Kong?"

"He couldn't. There's no paper trail that they were related. Marriage was the only option."

Raina nodded in agreement. And at the time and in a remote village, everyone blamed the victim. Made perfect sense. "But why did he keep this from Po Po and the rest of the family?"

Sonny shrugged. "You know how it is in Chinese families. It's always the victim's fault. One false move and you bring shame to your family for generations."

"I wondered if the entire thing—the job at the Ministry of Agriculture and the marriage—was my great-grandfather's doing," Raina said. It wouldn't surprise her if her great-grandfather had a hand in arranging everything. There was a reason he was known as a wily fox in the Wong side of the family.

"No, your great-grandfather never knew about the marriage. The half-sister wasn't his."

Raina's eyes widened in shock. Her great-grandma? In that generation, they still hogtied and threw "loose" wives into a river to prove their innocence. No wonder her grandfather had to marry the half-sister. He had to hide his mother's shame. And he couldn't betray his mother by telling Po Po. It would have brought shame to him too.

She sagged against the bed, and the doubt about her grandfather left her. He was the honorable man she had known her entire life. She blinked at the tears burning in the back of her eyes. She couldn't wait to tell Po Po.

"I'm sorry, but I need to talk to my grandma." Raina

jumped up from the bed. "She deserves to hear the truth."

"Whoa! Don't you want to know where the half-sister and the son are?" Sonny asked.

Raina swiveled her head like a ventriloquist. "Where are they?" she whispered. She had to bring them to San Francisco. She'd failed in her duty to send them money like her grandfather had wanted. Now she needed to make amends with them and bring them home.

Sonny handed her a slip of paper with an address on it. "Malaysia."

Raina's hand shook when she reached for the paper. "Th...thank you."

Sonny cupped her chin in his hand. "You have no idea how beautiful you look when you are this vulnerable." He kissed her, a brief brush of his soft lips on hers. Even then, she still grimaced at her stinging lips. The duct tape had done its job well.

When he left, Raina shook with emotion. She curled up in a fetal position and cried, not because her heart was broken, but because she should have trusted her heart.

Matthew came back a few minutes later. He took one look at her and scooped her up in his arms. Yep, everything was right in her world again.

THERE WAS something rather comfortable about being a passenger in a vehicle driven by someone Raina trusted above all else. Matthew drove with one hand on the steering wheel and the other holding her hand. The engagement ring threw sparks and possibilities in the space between them.

At some point, they should probably talk, but for now, Raina was more than happy to just be in the moment. The sun warmed her skin, and she took a deep hungry breath. To be alive was glorious.

"I checked up on Sonny Kwan with some friends of mine," Matthew said, breaking the silence between them. "The FBI caught up with him in San Francisco earlier this year. They won't tell me what happened but told me to leave Sonny alone."

"That's odd. You have access to the Kwan mansion. Why wouldn't they want your help to take down this crime boss?" Raina asked. Unless... "Is he working for them now?"

Matthew shook his head. "You're too smart for your own good. I suspect there's some kind of deal at work here, but let's pretend we're dumb and blind on this one."

Raina agreed with him. She didn't want to have anything else to do with Sonny Kwan and his world ever again.

Matthew pulled up to the gate at the Kwan mansion and spoke with the guard through the intercom. The gates opened, and Matthew started the drive up to the house.

Raina's cell phone dinged from inside her purse. She tapped on the screen to open her email and a goofy smile spread across her face. It was from Moody Investigations, and they wanted her to come in for an interview.

She glanced at Matthew and decided to share the news with him only if she got the job. No point in mentioning it if she didn't get the internship. She couldn't wait to tell her grandma the news though. They could do a celebratory dance together.

Before she could tuck her phone back into her purse, it dinged again. She frowned at the text message from her sister.

He glanced over. "Is everything okay?"

"I don't know. Her husband walked off with a travel bag two weeks ago and hasn't been in touch since."

"Were they having marital problems?"

"Not that I know of. He wouldn't walk away from his career. Leaving Cassie would be akin to slitting his own throat. Uncle Anthony would fire him immediately, and that would be the end of his law career in San Francisco."

He patted her knee. "We'll be back in the States soon. I'm sure it will turn out okay."

She glanced out the window at the video cameras recording their progress toward the mansion. "I hope so." Especially for her beloved niece's sake.

THE END

PLEASE REVIEW my books at your *retailer*. As an indie author, reviews help other readers find my books. I appreciate all reviews, whether positive or negative.

Continue Raina's story now.
Murky Passions and Scandals
(Raina Sun #6)

ACKNOWLEDGMENTS

A story is a dream that a writer brings to life on paper. But a book needs a team to nurture it into an enjoyable experience.

I want to thank my editors, Alicia S. and Sara P., for wrangling my words so they are coherent.

And then, there are my beta-readers—Marion D., Joyce S., Silva P., and the anonymous readers—thank you, ladies, for volunteering your time to catch these sneaky typos and grammatical errors.

Thanks, reader David B. for loaning me your name.

And finally, thank you, Susan C. for the awesome cover.

I wouldn't have been able to bring this story to life without all of you. —Anne R. Tan

ALSO BY ANNE R. TAN

Thanks for reading *Sunny Mates and Murders*. I hope you enjoyed it!

Want to know about new releases, sale pricing, and exclusive content?

Sign up for Anne R. Tan's email newsletter at http://annertan.com/newsletter

Your information would not be sold or transferred. Thank you for trusting me with your email.

Want More Raina Sun?

Raining Men and Corpses (Raina Sun #1)

Gusty Lovers and Cadavers (Raina Sun #2)

Breezy Friends and Bodies (Raina Sun #3)

Balmy Darlings and Death (Raina Sun #4)

Sunny Mates and Murders (Raina Sun #5)

Murky Passions and Scandals (Raina Sun #6)

Smoldering Flames and Secrets (Raina Sun #7)

Hazy Grooms and Homicides (Raina Sun #8)

Chilly Comforts and Disasters (Raina Sun #9)

Fair Cronies and Felonies (Raina Sun Mystery #10)

How about another series by Anne R. Tan?

Just Shoot Me Dead (Lucy Fong #1)

MURKY PASSIONS AND SCANDALS

Raina Sun knew she'd made a tactical error two minutes into the surveillance job for Moody Investigation's newest client. She'd asked her grandma to keep her company in this easy assignment. Since seven o'clock in the morning, Raina and Po Po had watched the Westchester home, a ten-thousand-square-foot monstrosity, from the comfort of Raina's thirteen-year-old car. It was only a quarter past nine, and she was ready to strangle her grandma.

Po Po popped the top of her second can of Red Bull. "How much longer will this take? Maybe we should barge into the home and rough her up a bit to get a confession."

Her grandma didn't need the caffeine. At seventy—wait, her grandma was sixty this week—and a little over five feet, Po Po was a ball of energy. Ever since they got back to California from Toronto a few months ago, her grandma had an extra spring in her step and more bounce in her hair—literally, since she turned her long silvery braid into a chin-length bob with pink streaks.

Raina rubbed her temple. This was the third outrageous suggestion in the last fifteen minutes. "There's no confession. We're only noting her activities while her husband is at work. There might not even be an affair."

"Of course there's an affair. First, he's old and rich," Po Po said, ticking the point off on her fingers. "She's young enough to be his granddaughter—"

"He's not old. He's only in his late fifties—"

"He probably needs to stock the little blue pill like toilet paper to keep her happy. It's that Latina blood. I bet you they have a fireman pole in the bedroom—"

Raina plugged her fingers into her ears. "La-la-la."

Po Po threw her hands up in the air. "You'll be a married woman soon. You need to hear these things so you can keep your man happy."

Raina sighed. If Matthew wanted a pole in their bedroom, she would tell him exactly where to put it. "Why don't we play the Quiet Game? The first person to speak loses." She mimed zipping up her lips and tossing away the key. Sometimes a kindergartner was more obliging than her grandma.

Po Po gave her an expression that said she was only biding her time. She rooted inside her large hobo bag that could double for a carry-on and probably held weapons of mass destruction. She pulled out her cell phone and tapped on the screen. Blessed silence filled the faded red Honda.

The surveillance job was Raina's first assignment without supervision. Sure it was minimum wage, but the hours counted as paid experience toward a private investigator license. It was simple enough to tail the client's third wife and document her affair. A little sleazy, yes, but it was much safer than a murder investigation.

Po Po held out her cell phone. "Your sister wants to talk to you."

Raina shook her head. "Not now. I'm on the job."

"You're not doing anything at the moment. She wants your help."

"I don't want to get in the middle of their marriage. If she wants to know what's going on with her husband, she should ask him."

Po Po's fingers flew across the screen, tapping out a text. Her phone chirped at the incoming message. "She said she'd pay you to play detective."

"I don't need her to pay me. I already have a job as a detective," Raina said. She sounded peevish, and she didn't like it. Her older sister always had a way of getting under her skin.

"She said—"

"Something is happening." Raina started her car and reached for her seatbelt. "Tell Cassie we'll get back to her later."

The carriage-style garage door of the McMansion rolled open, and a stunning Hispanic woman in her early thirties drove out in a black Mercedes-Benz SUV. Even from a distance, Raina could see the wide brown eyes and kissable pouty mouth on the oval face meant for a magazine. Some women had all the luck.

Not that Raina was jealous. After all, the curly black hair that made her look like a walking cotton candy on a stick was good enough to get her Matthew. And old age would add enough padding to her boyish figure, although it probably wouldn't be at desirable locations.

She snorted. Who was she kidding? Of course, she was slightly jealous, but it would all even out. In fifty years, time and gravity would make both of them look like the cute apple head dolls found at craft fairs.

Besides, there was trouble in paradise. Mia Westchester's husband wouldn't have hired a private investigator to tail her if all was well at the home front. She made a left out of the driveway and came toward them.

Raina flipped the visor down and pretended to check non-existent eye makeup in the mirror, partially blocking her face with her hand. Po Po ducked, squeezing her head between her knees. Mia paid them no attention and kept going. When the coast was clear, Raina signaled and made a U-turn to follow their quarry.

Po Po made a fist pump and bounced on her seat. "Showtime!"

"The husband only wants to document where she's going while he's at work. I don't think she's doing anything all that exciting," Raina said, secretly hoping she was wrong. The last few days had been a snooze fest.

"Hot and steamy! Hot and steamy!" Po Po chanted like a child wishing for a treat. "I hope she's doing the nasty with the cabana boy."

Raina wanted to slam her head on the steering wheel. Why did she think it was a good idea to include her grandma? Oh, right. So Po Po wouldn't feel neglected now that she had to share Raina's time with Matthew. Talk about juggling two big babies.

Five minutes later the SUV pulled into the parking lot of a medical office complex.

"See? She probably has a doctor's appointment," Raina said.

Po Po slumped back in her seat, disappointment written across her face.

Raina slowed and rolled past the driveway for a street side parking spot. From the rear view mirror, she saw a white van with dark windows pull up next to the SUV.

"Come on, cabana boy," Po Po said, twisting her upper body to look out the rear window. "Hey! A threesome. Oh, she's a super freak. I like her already."

Raina pulled up next to the curb, thankful she didn't have to deal with parallel parking. She whipped around to see what her grandma was crowing about.

Two Hispanic men with dark sunglasses and full beards—scruffy and definitely not cabana boy caliber—came out of the white van. They opened the SUV driver door and pulled the wife out of the vehicle. She screamed and threw a punch, but one man pinned her arms behind her.

"What's going on?" Po Po said, her voice full of alarm. "We have to do something."

Raina threw off her seatbelt and grabbed the pepper spray from her purse. "Call the police. She's being kidnapped," she called over her shoulder. She took off toward the van.

One man held the woman against his chest, and the other pressed a rag against her mouth. Within seconds she sagged and went limp. They tossed her effortlessly into the van and slammed the door shut.

The van driver pulled out of the parking lot, nearly plowing into a car pulling into the lot. The car's driver honked and cursed at the white van. The van driver gave him the bird and peeled out of the parking lot in a squeal of tires.

Raina pumped her arms and pushed a little harder. Even though she was in decent shape, she couldn't outrun a speeding vehicle. Her lungs burned, and her breath came out in loud puffs.

"Duck!" Po Po hollered from behind.

Raina dropped to the ground.

Wha-amp! Wha-amp!

Air rushed past Raina. She lifted her head to see mini pumpkins smacking into the bumper and splattering onto the road. The white van swayed into oncoming traffic and over-corrected itself, sideswiping the parked vehicles.

Wha-amp!

The mini pumpkin missed its target, hit the parked green car by the curb, and splattered onto the road. The white van hooked a right and disappeared from view.

Raina got up and jogged back to her grandma. Po Po lowered a small cylindrical metal tube from her shoulder. Where did her grandma get the homemade pumpkin launcher? And how did she fit it into her bag?

"In the car. Let's go," Raina said, hopping in and turning on the engine. She made an illegal U-turn and chased after the white van, taking the right turn too wide for her comfort.

Po Po held onto the handle above the window, the pumpkin launcher cradled between her knees. With her other hand, she dug out her bird watching binoculars from her purse. "Six. Alpha. Foxtrot. Papa. One. Four. Two," she called out the license plate's numbers. "I'll memorize the letters, and you'll memorize the numbers."

Raina nodded. "Okay. One-two-four."

"One-four-two," Po Po corrected, tossing the binoculars back into her bag. She leaned out the window and settled the pumpkin launcher between her shoulder and ear.

"What do you think you're doing?" Raina said, reaching across the center console to hold onto the elastic waistband of her grandma's jeans. "Sit down, Po Po. You'll fall out of the car, and I can't drive with one hand holding onto your behind."

"Just give me one shot." Her grandma aimed and pulled the trigger. A mini pumpkin launched out of the tube and missed the van.

The van driver slammed on the brakes and hooked a left, almost getting into a head-on collision with traffic from the opposite lane.

Raina pulled up to the next intersection to make a legal U-turn. By the time she got to the street where she'd last seen the white van, it was long gone—along with the woman she was paid to tail.

When Raina and Po Po returned to the crime scene, they found Officer Joanna Hopper pacing the parking lot, inspecting the asphalt. Her police cruiser was parked next to the curb behind the green car with a dent from the pumpkin launcher. If they squinted, the golf ball-size dent wasn't noticeable.

"How are we to explain the mini pumpkins? Do we need to leave our insurance information for the green car?" Raina asked her grandma.

Po Po tucked the pumpkin launcher back into her purse. She put a finger to her lips. "Shhhh. No one has to know. Collateral damage is to be expected."

"But what about the green car?"

Po Po pulled out an envelope from her purse and waved it in the air. "There's enough money in here to cover the damage. Spillman Insurance is helping me find a new umbrella policy. The last one canceled mine." She rolled her eyes. "Apparently I put in too many claims."

"But shouldn't we at least leave a note with the money?"

"Got that covered too. There's a canned letter inside, apologizing for the damage, and some cash to cover the repair bill." Po Po beamed. "Am I smart or what?"

Raina ignored the question. It was a fantastic solution to an awkward situation. No name and phone numbers to leave behind. But what little old granny walked around with pre-written apology notes and cash in an envelope? "How many of these envelopes do you have in your purse?"

"Not that many. I'm down to one now. I'll have to get back to the condo soon so I can replenish."

"Po Po, is it safe to be walking around with this much money?"

"It's just a temporary solution until I can get another policy. I have full faith in Spillman Insurance." Po Po tucked the envelope back inside her purse. "I'll leave the note after the policewoman leaves. I don't want her asking questions. I'm not sure my new toy is, uh...legal."

Raina groaned inwardly. She didn't even want to start on the subject of legality with her grandma. "Where did you get it?"

"The high school kids built it for me. I offered a five-hundred-dollar scholarship to the team who could make it small enough to fit into my bag."

Raina could imagine what the family would say if her grandma got hauled into the police station for corrupting the youths in town. "We better go over to Officer Hopper before she comes over here. I don't want her to see your new toy."

They got out of Raina's faded red Honda Accord and trotted toward the officer. People came out of the office building and got into their cars, probably going out for lunch. Surprisingly, they only gave Officer Hopper a passing glance.

"The only suspicious thing I see is the splattered mini pumpkin on the street," Officer Hopper said, hands on her hips. She was older than Raina, probably thirty years old. Her blonde hair was pulled back in a tight French braid, and her flinty gray eyes regarded the two of them like they were a couple of pranksters.

Raina gave her grandma a sideways glance. Po Po put on her best senile senior citizen look, her eyes at half-mast and unfocused. At moments like this, Raina wanted nothing more than to call her grandma out.

Suppressing a sigh, Raina addressed the police officer. "We saw a woman get kidnapped in this parking lot. Her name is Mia Westchester."

"Is this a joke?" Officer Hopper said, glancing at Po Po. "This is not the first time the senior citizens in this town have led me on a wild goose chase."

Po Po blinked like she wasn't the ringleader for these previous operations to get even with the officer who was once Raina's romantic rival. "We have the license plate number for the van." She rattled it off.

Officer Hopper pulled out a notebook and wrote down the license plate number. "I'll run this through the system." Her tone sounded bored like she was indulging them.

Raina walked over to Mia's car and glanced inside. The keys dangled from the ignition, and her purse was in the passenger seat. "If she wasn't kidnapped, how do you explain her keys and purse in the car?"

Officer Hopper came over and glanced inside. Her expression morphed from annoyance to alarm. "I'm calling for backup."

The next two hours flew by in a blur. They were questioned and re-questioned, more police officers came and went, walkie-talkies crackled with life and fell into silence, and her grandma complained about missing lunch. They were finally thanked for their time and dismissed. In other words, the police would take over from here.

Raina and Po Po headed for the Venus Café. Depending on who you talked to in town, the café was either a welcoming gathering place or an abomination. It was unassuming on the outside—an olive green bungalow with white trim—but like everything else in life, it was the inside that showed the world who you really were.

The Venus Café had floor-to-ceiling murals of handsome men frolicking with the Greek goddess in the woods. Only strategically placed flowing hair or bits of leaves kept the paintings in the art category. Raina always felt a secret thrill when she stepped into the café. It was good to be a little naughty even if it was vicariously through painted women.

It was two thirty, which meant the senior citizen crowd would be drifting in for the early bird dinner soon.

One of Po Po's friends was already there, reading in a cracked leather chair by the large fireplace.

Brenda Sullivan, the owner, was wiping a table when they came in. "Your usual?" she asked, pulling a notepad from the pocket of her apron.

"I am so hungry I could eat my foot. No senior portion for me this time," Po Po said, dropping into a chair at the adjacent table.

The café owner raised an eyebrow and glanced at Raina. "Difficult morning?"

"You can say that again. There was a kidnapping, and then we got into a high-speed car chase," Po Po said. She took a deep breath. "And—"

"A roast beef sandwich on sourdough and a large ice caramel macchiato," Raina cut in. "Please put our order in the kitchen first."

Brenda tore the order slip from the notepad and headed toward the kitchen. "I'll be right back." Half a minute later she settled herself across from Po Po. "So who got kidnapped?"

As Raina listened to her grandma launch into the tale, an uneasy feeling settled in her stomach that had nothing to do with food. The three of them had discussed other cases in the past, but this Westchester case was different. Even though Raina trusted Brenda to not talk about this case with anyone else, she was still breaching a client's privacy.

What if she could no longer discuss her cases with anyone? She didn't think being a private detective meant she would end up a lone wolf seeking justice for her clients. This private investigator business was more complicated than she had envisioned.

Her grandma mimed using her homemade pumpkin launcher. "And then—"

"Brenda," Raina interrupted. "Could you pack my lunch to go? I need to get back to the office." As long as she wasn't here, she technically wasn't discussing her client's case. Besides, she should probably tell her boss about the kidnapping before she heard it from someone else.

"Do you want me to go with you?" Po Po asked. Her tone implied she was only asking out of politeness.

Raina shook her head. She knew her grandma couldn't wait to get back to the senior center to tell her cronies about her great escapade this morning. "I'll probably have to file a report and call our client."

"What are you going to tell the husband?" Brenda asked.

"I don't know. It depends on whether or not the police called him yet," Raina said.

"What are you going to tell your new boss?" Po Po asked.

Raina grimaced. "I don't know."

"Well, at least she can't blame you for this," Brenda said. "It's not like you had anything to do with the kidnapping."

While Raina might've had nothing to do with the kidnapping, she couldn't help but worry about Arthur Westchester's reaction when he found out his wife was kidnapped right in front of Raina's eyes.

Join the fun. Buy now.
Murky Passions and Scandals
(Raina Sun #6)

ABOUT THE AUTHOR

Anne R. Tan fell in love with storytelling in elementary school, but decided to study engineering so she could get a "real job." Her day job is her vacation from home and she moonlights as a writer to keep the voices inside her head under control.

Her cozy mysteries feature Raina Sun, a Chinese American amateur sleuth, on the cusp of change in her life. Not only is she dealing with finding love and overcoming family betrayals, she is also solving murders.

If you are interested in learning more about Tan and her writing process, sign up for Anne R. Tan's email newsletter at http://annertan.com/newsletter for exclusive content, new release announcements, and sales.

www.ingramcontent.com/pod-product-compliance
Lightning Source LLC
Chambersburg PA
CBHW050358190726
48284CB00007BB/2342